D0048751

Mystery Stories

Other titles by Enid Blyton in Armada

The Naughtiest Girl Again
The Rockingdown Mystery
The Rubadub Mystery
The Rilloby Fair Mystery
The Ring O'Bells Mystery
The Rat-a-tat Mystery
The Secret of Killimooin
The Secret Mountain
The Secret of Spiggy Holes
The Secret of Moon Castle
The Six Bad Boys
The Put-Em-Rights
Six Cousins at Mistletoe Farm
Six Cousins Again
Those Dreadful Children
The Family at Red-Roofs
The Children at Green Meadows

Coming soon in Armada

Adventure Stories

Enid Blyton

MYSTERY STORIES

The Secret of Cliff Castle

and

Smuggler Ben

Armada

The Secret of Cliff Castle and *Smuggler Ben*
were first published separately
in 1947 and 1943 respectively
by T. Werner Laurie Ltd.
First published in the U.K. in hardback in this edition
in 1976 by
William Collins Sons & Co. Ltd.,
London and Glasgow.
First published in Armada in 1982 by
Fontana Paperbacks,
14 St. James's Place, London SW1A 1PS.

Printed in Great Britain by
Love & Malcomson Ltd.,
Brighton Road, Redhill, Surrey.

THE SECRET OF
CLIFF CASTLE

CONTENTS

CHAPTER 1

OFF FOR A HOLIDAY

PETER AND Pam leaned out of the railway carriage together and waved good-bye to their mother as their train slowly left the long platform.

" Good-bye, Mother! Good-bye! "

" Be good! " called Mother. " Good-bye! Have a lovely holiday! Give my love to Auntie Hetty."

" I hope Brock will be at the station to meet us," said Peter. " Good old Brock. It will be lovely to see his round, smiling face again."

Brock was their cousin. They were going to stay with him for part of the summer holidays, down in the country village of Rockhurst. Usually they went to the sea, but this summer Mother thought it would be nice for them to be in the country. Then Auntie Hetty had written to invite them for three weeks, and the children had been thrilled.

"We can go to the farm and see all the new animals there," said Pam. "And we can go exploring in the woods and find exciting things there. I hope there are some woods near."

"There are always woods in the country," said Peter. "Anyway, Brock will know all the places to go to. It's fun going to a place we've never been to before!"

The train sped on. It soon left London behind, and green fields took the place of houses and streets. The train was an express, and stopped at very few stations. The children had sandwiches with them, and when Pam's wrist-watch showed half-past twelve, Peter undid the parcel Mother had handed them, and took out the packets of food.

"I always feel so hungry in a train, somehow," said Pam. "Oooh—ham sandwiches. How lovely! What's in that other packet, Peter?"

"Biscuits, and two pieces of cake," said Peter, looking to see. "Oh, and two bars of chocolate as well. What a nice lunch. Mother's put in some lemonade, too—it's in that bag, Pam. Get it down."

Pam reached down the leather bag, in which Mother had squeezed a bottle of lemonade and two cardboard cups. Soon the two children were eating a lovely lunch, watching the scenery as it flew by the carriage window.

"We shall arrive at Rockhurst at half-past

three," said Peter. "But we've got to change at Deane. We must look out for that."

It was quite easy to change at Deane. A porter came by, calling, "Change here for Rockhurst! Change here for Rockhurst," and out the children hopped with their suit-cases. The little train for Rockhurst stood on the other side of the platform, and they simply got out of one train and into the other! It was fun.

"Shan't be long now," said Peter. "You know, Pam, I feel awfully excited. I feel as if we're going to have adventures!"

"I feel that too," said Pam. "But I usually do feel like that when I'm setting out on a holiday."

"So do I" said Peter. "But this time I feel we really are. Proper adventures, I mean. Sort of dangerous, you know!"

"Do you really?" said Pam, feeling all excited too. "Oooh, I hope we do have some. I'd like some. School was so dull last term that I could do with something exciting in the hols!"

"Goodness! Isn't it slow, after the express!" said Pam. "We could almost lean out of the window and pick flowers off the bank!"

Peter laughed. "Well, in another twenty minutes we shall be there," he said. "And then we'll see old Brock."

The time went by, and at exactly half-past three the little train drew in at a small country platform, where red geraniums flared in beds at the back. "Rockhurst!" shouted the one and only porter. "ROCKHURST!"

Peter jumped out, and helped Pam down. She looked eagerly up and down the platform, whilst Peter dragged out the two suit-cases and the big leather bag. Pam gave a shriek.

" Oh! There's Brock! Brock! Brock! Here we are! Hallo! "

Brock came rushing up. He was a tall boy, with a strong body, and a red, smiling face. His eyes shone very blue in the sunshine as he greeted his cousins. He was twelve, the same age as Peter, but stronger and taller. Pam was eleven, smaller than either of the boys.

Brock clapped his cousins on the back, and grinned at them. " Hallo! Glad to see you both! Welcome to Rockhurst! "

" Hallo! " said Peter, smiling. " It's fine to see you, Brock. Golly, you've grown awfully tall since we saw you last year. You make me quite feel small."

" Come on," said Brock, taking one of the suit-cases. " Mother's outside with the pony-cart. It'll just about take us all, though we'll have to put our feet on these cases."

They gave up their tickets, and went out of the station, chattering hard. Pam called out to her aunt, in delight, " Hallo, Aunt Hetty! Here we are! It is nice of you to come and meet us."

" Hallo, my dears," said their aunt. " Glad to see you. Climb into the cart. Brock, hand up the cases first, and I'll pack them under our feet."

Soon the four of them were driving swiftly along the country lanes. Sally, the pony, was a smart little beast, and cantered along merrily. The sun shone down, and everything looked gay and holiday-like. The children felt very happy.

They soon arrived at Brock's home. It was a comfortable-looking house, rather rambling, set in a nice big garden. The children liked the look of it very much.

" It's a friendly sort of house, isn't it? " said Pam. " Oh, Aunt Hetty, isn't the beginning of a holiday exciting? "

" Very exciting! " said their aunt. " Quite the most exciting part of a holiday, I always think."

" But it isn't going to be the most exciting part of *this* holiday! " said Peter, as the pony trotted in at the gate and came to a standstill in front of the house. " I've got a funny feeling about this holiday. It's going to be exciting all the way through! "

" What do you mean? " asked Brock, in surprise.

" I don't exactly know," said Peter, jumping down, and helping his aunt out. " But I've got a Feeling! You just wait and see! "

" Well, I hope your Feeling is right! " said Brock, and they all went into the house.

CHAPTER 2

A LITTLE EXPLORING

TEA WAS ready when they got indoors. The children washed their hands and brushed their hair. Peter was sharing Brock's little room, and Pam had a tiny room to herself up in the attic. She loved it because it had queer, slanting ceilings, and funny, uneven boards in the floor. She looked out of the window as she brushed her hair, humming a little tune to herself because she was so happy.

The countryside lay smiling in the afternoon sunshine. Cottages clustered together here and there, and cattle grazed in the fields. In the distance, a curious, steep hill caught her eye. It rose up very suddenly, and at the top was a strange building. It looked like a small, square castle, for it had towers at each end.

"I wonder if anyone lives there," thought Pam. "It looks sort of deserted, somehow. I'll ask Brock about it."

Downstairs, round the tea-table, Brock and his cousins chattered nineteen to the dozen about everything, telling each other all their news. Aunt Hetty smiled as she listened, and handed round her plates of home-made scones with jam, and new ginger buns, and currant pasties.

"Anyone would think you hadn't had anything to eat since breakfast-time," she said, as one after another the plates were emptied.

"Well, we did have a good lunch on the train," said Peter, "but it seems ages ago now. I do like these buns, Aunt Hetty. They're the nicest I've ever tasted."

"Shall we go out and explore round a bit, after tea?" said Pam. "I'm longing to. I saw the farm not far off, Brock—and what is that strange sort of castle on the top of that very steep hill towards the west?"

"Oh, that's Cliff Castle," said Brock. "It's called that because it's built on that steep hill, which falls away behind the castle in a kind of cliff."

"Does anyone live there?" asked Peter.

"Not now," said Brock. "Mother, who lived there, years ago?"

"Oh, I don't really know," said Mother. "It

belonged to a queer old man who wanted to live quite alone. So he built himself that castle, and lived there with two old servants, as queer as himself. He spent a fortune on the castle. When he died, he left a will which said the castle was to be left exactly as it was, cared for by the two old servants till they died. Then it was to go to some great-nephew, who has never bothered to live there—or even to go and visit the castle, as far as I know."

" Is it really a castle? " said Pam.

" No, not really," said Aunt Hetty. " But it's built to appear like one, as you see—and I believe the walls are almost as thick as a real old castle's would be. People do say that there are secret passages in it, but I don't believe that. What would a lonely old man want with secret passages! That's just make-believe."

The children stared out of the window at the lonely castle on the top of the steep hill. It suddenly seemed very mysterious and exciting to them. It stood there, with the sinking sun behind it, and looked rather black and forbidding.

" Is it quite empty then, Aunt Hetty? " asked Pam.

" Quite," said her aunt. " It must be in a dreadful mess by now, too, I should think, for nobody has dusted it for years, or lighted a fire there to warm the place. The furniture must be mouldy and rotten. Not a nice place to visit at all! "

Peter and Pam looked at one another. It seemed to them that their aunt was quite wrong. It would be a wonderfully exciting place to visit! If only they could!

After tea, they spoke to Brock about it. " Brock! Will you take us to see Cliff Castle one day soon? To-morrow, perhaps. It does sound so exciting— and it looks so strange and lonely. We'd simply love to explore round about it."

" We'll go to-morrow! " said Brock. " But come and see our garden now—and the farm. We've plenty of time."

So the three of them went over Brock's big garden, and admired the vegetables, the outdoor tomatoes, the peaches on the wall, and everything. They saw Brock's exciting play-house in the garden, too, set all by itself out of sight of the house.

" Daddy had this built for me to take my friends to, when we wanted to play by ourselves," said Brock. " You know, Mother doesn't like a lot of noise, and boys can't help being rowdy, can they? So I just take my friends to my play-house when we want a good old game—and we don't disturb Mother a bit! We can play out here on rainy days, too. It will be fun."

Peter and Pam liked Brock's play-house. It was a small, sturdy, little wooden house with a red door, and windows each side. Inside there was one big room, and around it were spread all Brock's possessions—a small gramophone, a big meccano set, boxes and boxes of railway lines, engines, trucks, signals, and other things belonging to a railway—and on a bookshelf were scores of exciting-looking books.

" You *are* lucky, Brock! " said Peter, looking round. " This is a lovely place."

" Yes—we'll come here and talk when we want to be all by ourselves," said Brock. " Nobody can see us or hear us. It's our own private place."

They went to see the farm, too—and then the sun sank so low that it was time to go back home to supper. The strange castle on the hill showed up clearly as they went down the farm-lane back to their house.

" Brock, do take us to Cliff Castle to-morrow," said Peter. " It would really be marvellous fun to explore it. Haven't you ever been there yourself? "

" I haven't been very near it," said Brock. " I somehow never liked the look of it very much, you know. I think it's got rather a wicked look! "

" It has, rather," said Peter. " Anyway, do let's go to-morrow! "

" All right," said Brock. " I shan't mind going with you—though I've never wanted to go alone! "

It was fun going to bed that night in a strange bedroom. The two boys talked till late, and Brock's mother had to go in twice to stop them. Pam could hear their voices as she lay in bed, and she wished she was with the two boys so that she might hear what they said.

She fell asleep, and did not wake until the house was all in a bustle with its early-morning cleaning. She heard the two boys talking below in loud voices, and she jumped out of bed at once.

" It's holiday-time—and we're at Brock's—and we're going exploring to-day! " she hummed to herself, as she dressed quickly. She ran downstairs to breakfast feeling very hungry.

"What are you going to do to-day?" asked Aunt Hetty, pouring out the tea.

"We're going over to Cliff Castle," said Brock. "Can we take sandwiches, Mother, and have a picnic?"

"All right," said his mother. "You must all make your beds, and tidy your rooms, please, before you go. I'll get you some lunch ready whilst you do that."

It wasn't long after breakfast before the three children were ready to set out. Brock's mother had been very generous with the picnic lunch. She had cut them potted meat sandwiches, tomato sandwiches, and egg sandwiches, and had put some buttered scones, some ginger buns, and some boiled sweets into the packets too.

"There's a tiny shop, not far from Cliff Castle, where you can buy yourselves something to drink," she said. "Here is some money for that. Now—off you go!"

They set off happily. Brock knew the way, though it was rather a roundabout one, down narrow little lanes, through a small wood, and then across some fields. It was eleven o'clock by the time they got to the little shop where they wanted to buy drinks.

"I'm so thirsty already that I could drink about twelve bottles of lemonade straight off!" said Peter.

"Well, don't let's drink all of it straight away,"

said Brock. " The woman here has a well—look, there it is, with the bucket beside it. Let's ask her if we can have a drink of cold water—then we can save up the lemonade! "

The woman said that of course they could use her well-water. " Have a whole bucketful, if you like! " she said. But they couldn't quite manage that. They sent down the bucket, and it came up filled with silvery water.

" It's absolutely ice-cold! " said Pam, gasping a little at the coldness. " But it's simply lovely."

" Where are you off to? " asked the woman, handing out three small bottles of lemonade.

" To explore round about Cliff Castle," said Peter.

" Oh, I wouldn't do that," said the woman. " Really, I wouldn't. It's a queer place. And people do say that funny lights have been seen there lately. Well, that's very strange, isn't it, in a place that's been empty for years? "

" Very queer," said Brock, staring at the woman, and feeling rather excited. " What sort of lights? "

" I don't know," said the woman. " I only know I wouldn't go near that place in the dark, or in the daytime either! There's always been something queer about it—and there is still! "

The children said good-bye and went out of the tiny, dark shop. They stared up at the nearby hill, on the top of which stood Cliff Castle. It looked much bigger now that they were near it. It had funny little slit-like windows, just like very old castles had. It certainly was a queer place for anyone to build in days when castles were no longer of any use!

"Well, come on," said Brock, at last. "Don't let's be put off by silly village-stories. Mother says stories always get made up about any deserted place."

"They certainly make it more exciting," said Peter, hitching his kit-bag full of lunch over his other shoulder. "Well—up the hill we go!"

And up the hill they went. There was no proper road up the steep hill, only a small, narrow path that wound between jutting-out rocks, for it was a very rocky part of the countryside. Stunted bushes grew on the hillside, mostly of gorse. It was exposed to the east winds, and nothing very much grew there.

"Well—here we are!" said Brock at last. "Cliff Castle! I wonder what we shall find there!"

CHAPTER 3

CLIFF CASTLE

Now THAT the children were right up to the castle, it looked enormous! It rose up in front of them, square and sturdy, a tower at each end. Its small, slit-like windows had no glass in. The great front door was studded with big nails that had gone rusty. There was a large knocker, which the children longed to use—but which, of course, they dared not touch!

"Let's go all the way round the castle and see what we can see," said Pam.

So they went down the great flight of steps again, and began to make their way round the towering

24

walls of the strange castle. It was difficult, because creepers, bushes and weeds grew high up the walls. Tall nettles stood in great patches, and the children had to make their way round them after Pam was badly stung on her bare legs.

" We'll find some dock leaves to help the stings," said Peter, and he found a patch of dark green dock leaves. He picked some and Pam pressed the cool leaves against her burning skin.

" That's better," she said. " Gracious, I shan't go near nettles again to-day! "

They went on their way round the great grey walls. The slit-like windows were placed at regular intervals. The children gazed up at them.

" You know, in the olden days, they had those funny narrow windows so that archers could shoot their arrows out without being hit themselves," said Brock, rather learnedly. " I can't imagine why the old man should have built windows like that for himself, long after the time of bows and arrows had gone! It must make the rooms inside awfully dark."

" I wish we could see them, don't you? " said Pam excitedly. " Just imagine how queer they would look after all these years when nobody has been here—cobwebs all over the place—dust everywhere. Oooh—it would be awfully queer."

They could not go all round the castle, because, when they came to the side that faced due west, the hill fell away so steeply that it was impossible to go any farther. The walls of the castle were built almost sheer with the hillside, and there was a very big drop down to the bottom of the hills below.

" Let's have our lunch now," said Peter, all at once feeling terribly hungry. " It's almost time. We can find a nice place out of the hot sun and sit down, can't we? "

" Rather! " said Brock, feeling hungry too. " Look—what about that shady bit over there, facing the castle? We can look at the queer castle whilst we're eating."

They sat down in the shady spot, and undid all they had to eat. It had seemed a lot when Brock's mother had packed it up—but it didn't seem nearly so much when three hungry children began to eat it. They unscrewed the tops of the lemonade bottles, and drank eagerly. Except that the lemonade tasted a little warm, it was delicious.

Pam finished her lunch first, because she did not want so much as the boys, and gave some of hers to them to finish up. She lay back against a tree and looked up at the silent grey castle.

She looked at the queer narrow windows and began to count them. When she came to the second row, she spoke out loud:

" Look, Peter; look, Brock—there's a window in the second row upwards that is bigger than the others. I wonder why."

The boys looked up. Peter screwed up his eyes to see why the window should be bigger.

" I don't think it's meant to be bigger," he said at last. " I think the weather has sort of eaten it away. It looks to me as if the bottom part of it has crumbled away. Perhaps a pipe comes out just there, and has leaked down the window and made the stone and brickwork rotten."

" Do you see the tree that grows up to that window? " said Brock, in sudden excitement. " I believe we could climb it and look in at that window! I wonder what we should see if we did! "

Peter and Pam stared at him, and then at the tree that grew up to the window. What fun it would be if they really could climb it and have a peep inside the castle!

" Well, let's see if we can peep inside any of the lower windows first," said Peter. " I don't think Aunt Hetty would be awfully pleased with us if we climbed trees in these clothes. We really want old clothes for that."

" Oh, bother our clothes! " said Brock, his red face shining with excitement. " I vote we climb up! But we'll have a peep in at one of the lower windows first. Peter, you come and give me a leg-up."

It wasn't long before Peter was bending down, heaving Brock up to the narrow window-sill to see inside the slit-like window. Brock peered through, but could see nothing at all.

" It's so dark inside," he said. " It wouldn't be so bad if the sun wasn't so brilliant to-day—but my eyes just simply can't see a thing inside the darkness of the castle."

" Well, we'll climb the tree then! " cried Pam, running to it. She loved climbing trees as much as the boys did.

" Wait a bit, Pam," cried Brock. " Peter and I will go up first, and give you a hand. You're only a girl, you know."

It always made Pam cross to be told she was only a girl. " I'm as strong as you are, anyway! " she cried, and looked about for an easy way to climb.

But Brock was up the tree before either of the others. He was a country boy, used to climbing, and he saw at once the best way to go up. He was soon lost to sight among the greenery.

His voice came down to them: " Go up the way I did. It's not difficult."

Peter followed him, and then Pam. Pam had to have a hand from Peter every now and again, and she was glad of it. They were soon all of them up on a high branch beside Brock. He grinned at them.

" Good climbing! " he said. " Now, look—see this branch? It reaches right to that window. It's pretty strong, and I think it will bear us all. But we'd better go one at a time, in case it doesn't."

" You go first, then," said Peter. Brock edged his way along the branch, working carefully with his arms and legs. The bough bent beneath his weight and swung down below the window-sill. Brock came back.

" No good," he said. " We'll try the next branch. That looks a good deal stronger—and although it grows right above the window at its tip, our weight will bend it down till it rests almost on the window-sill, I should think."

They all climbed a little higher. Then Brock worked his way along the next branch. As he said, his weight bent it gradually down, and by the time he was at the end of it, its tip rested on the sill itself. Part of it even went right through the window-opening into the castle.

" Fine! " said Brock. He put one leg across the stone window-sill, and peered into the slit. He could see nothing but darkness. But certainly the weather had worn away the stone around that window, for the opening was almost big enough to take Brock's stout body!

" I believe I could get right inside! " he called to the others. He stood upright on the sill and tried to work his way in. It was a very tight fit, for Brock was not thin! He had to squeeze himself in till he almost burst.

He found that the wall was very thick—about a yard thick, before he had got right through the window. Then he jumped down to the floor inside and called out through the slit:

" Come on! It's not very difficult! We'll be able to explore the castle from top to bottom, if you can get through! "

CHAPTER 4

INSIDE THE CASTLE

PAM FELT a little nervous about going right into
the castle, but she couldn't hold back if the boys
thought it was all right. So she followed Peter
when he squeezed himself through the slit in the
stone walls, and held his hand tightly when he
gave it to her to help her to jump down into the
darkness.

Two slit-like windows lighted the room they
were in. It seemed as dark as night to the children
when they first looked round—but their eyes soon
grew accustomed to it, and they began to see quite
well. Shafts of bright sunlight lighted up the room
in two places—the rest seemed rather dark.

They stared round, and then Pam cried out in disappointment:

"Oh—the room is empty! It's just like a prison cell! There's absolutely nothing here!"

She was right. There was nothing to see at all, except for bare walls, bare floor, and bare ceiling. At the far side was a closed door, big and strong. It had an iron handle. Brock went over to it.

"Well, we may be unlucky in this room, finding nothing to see," he said, "but maybe there will be plenty to see somewhere else! Let's open this door and explore!"

He pulled at the door by the great iron handle. It opened! Outside was a dark passage. Brock felt in his pockets, remembering that he had a torch somewhere. He found it, and switched it on.

The passage led from a narrow stone stairway, and seemed to wind round a corner. "Come on," said Brock. "This way! We'll open a few doors and see what there is to be seen."

He opened a door nearby. But again there was nothing to be seen but bareness. He shut the door, and the noise echoed through the stone castle in a very queer way. It sounded as though dozens of doors were being shut, one after another. Pam shivered.

"Oooh!" she said. "It's not nice to make a noise in this place. Even a little sound echoes round like thunder."

No room just there had anything in it at all. It was most disappointing. Brock then led the way to the stone staircase. It wound downwards in the heart of the castle, and as it came towards the bottom, grew a little wider.

It ended in a vast room with an enormous fireplace at one end. "This must be the kitchen," said Pam, in surprise. "And I suppose those stairs we came down were the back stairs. There must be a bigger flight somewhere else. I did think they were very narrow stairs for such a huge castle."

The kitchen was furnished. There was a big wooden table, and around it were set stout wooden chairs. Pots and pans hung around the stove. There was an iron pot hanging over what had once been a fire. Brock peered into it. There was an evil-smelling, dark liquid in it.

"Something made by witches!" he said, in a deep, mournful voice that made Pam jump. Brock laughed. "It's all right," he said. "It's only some soup, or something gone bad after all these years!"

The kitchen was dark and dirty, and there was not much to be seen there. The children went out of it and came into a great hall from which four doors led off. Brock opened one.

And then, indeed, there was something to be seen! The big room beyond the door was furnished most magnificently! Great couches, carved chairs, cabinets, tables—all these stood about the room just as they had been left! But how mournful they looked, for they were adorned with great spiders' webs, and when the children walked into the room, clouds of fine grey dust flew up from their feet.

Sunlight came in long golden shafts through four of the slit-like windows, and divided the room into quarters. It made the whole room even queerer than it might have been, for the brilliance of the sunlight lay in sharp contrast to the blackness of the shadows in the far corners.

"Oooh! What an enormous spider!" said Pam, with a shudder, as a great eight-legged spider ran out from under a table. The boys didn't mind spiders. They didn't even mind walking into the cobwebs that hung here and there from the enormous chandeliers that had once held dozens of candles to light the room. But Pam couldn't bear the strange, light touch of the webs on her hair, and longed to get out into the sunshine again.

"Isn't it queer, to have left everything just like this?" said Brock wonderingly. "Look at those curtains. They must once have been simply gorgeous—but now they are all faded and dusty."

He touched one—and it fell to pieces in his hand. It was almost as if someone had breathed on it and made it melt!

"The brocade on the furniture is all rotten, too," said Pam, as she felt it. It shredded away under her fingers. "Everything is moth-eaten. What a horrid, sad place this feels. I don't like it. Let's get away."

"No—we'll explore first," said Peter. "Don't be a spoil-sport, Pam. Come with us. You'll be quite all right."

Pam didn't want to be a spoil-sport, so she followed the boys rather unwillingly as they went out of the room and into the next.

The same things were found there—furniture

and curtains, rotten and decayed. A musty smell hung over everything. It was most unpleasant. Pam began to feel sick.

" I hate this smell," she said, " and I hate walking into these horrid webs. I can't seem to see them and it's horrid to get them all round my head."

" Let's go upstairs again," said Brock. " And this time we'll go up by the main stairway—look, that great flight of steps over there—not by the little narrow back staircase we came down."

They mounted the enormous stone steps, and came to some big rooms furnished as bedrooms. Up they went again and came to more rooms. Leading out of one of them was a tiny staircase all on its own. It wound up into one of the stone towers that stood at the end of the castle.

" Let's go up this staircase! " cried Peter. " We shall get a marvellous view over the countryside! "

So up they went and came to the open door of a strange, square little room that seemed to be cut right out of the heart of the tower. A tiny slit on each side lighted it. A stone bench ran round the walls, but otherwise there was nothing in the room.

" What a wonderful view! " cried Pam, peering out of one of the slits. She saw the whole of the countryside to the east lying smiling in the hot August sun. It looked marvellous.

" I can see our house! " cried Brock. " Over there, beyond the farm. Oh, how tiny it looks! And how small the cows and horses look, too. Like animals on a toy farm."

So they did. It was fun to peer out and see everything from so high up. But soon the children grew tired of it and thought they would go downstairs again.

So down they went, and then paused on the first floor where they had first squeezed in through the window. But somehow they couldn't find the room they had climbed inside! It was strange. They opened door after door, but no, there wasn't a tree outside a window.

" I've lost my bearings," said Peter at last. " I've no idea where that room was. Well, if we don't want to stay here all night we've got to get out somehow! I vote we go right downstairs into the hall, then make our way to the kitchen, and up that back stairway again. We know the room was somewhere near the top of that."

So down they went, into the hall, into the kitchen, and then towards the back stairway.

But just near the stairway was a small door, very low, set in the wall. The children stared at it. They hadn't noticed it before.

" Perhaps we could open this and get out by it," said Peter. " It would save us all that big climb down the tree. I tried the front door to see if we could get out by that, but it was much too heavy. The bolts had all rusted into the door, and I couldn't even turn the handle. Let's try this funny little door."

" It's so low we'll have to bend down to get out of it! " said Brock with a laugh. They went to the little door and looked at it. It was latched on the

. . . *Just near the stairway was a small door* . . .

inside, but not bolted or locked, though the key stood in the door. Peter lifted the latch.

After a push, the door opened a little way, and then stuck fast. The two boys together pushed hard. It opened just a little farther, and sunshine came through.

Peter put his head round the edge. "There's a great patch of nettles and a gorse bush preventing it from opening," he said. "Got a knife, Brock? I believe if I hacked away at this gorse bush a bit I could make the door open enough to let us out!"

Brock passed him a fierce-looking knife. Peter hacked at the bush, and cut off the pieces that were stopping the door from opening.

"Cut away the nettles, too," begged Pam. "My legs still sting from that other patch we went into."

Peter did his best. Then he and Brock were able to push the door open just enough to let them squeeze through one by one. They were all rather glad to be standing out in the bright sunshine again, after the dim, musty darkness of the silent castle.

"I say—if we just push this door to, and leave it like that, not locked or bolted, we shall be able to get in whenever we want to!" said Peter. "We might find it rather fun to come and play smugglers or something here. We could pile weeds against the door so that nobody else would notice it."

"Good idea!" said Brock. So they shut the door gently, then forced the gorse bush back against it, and pulled pieces from a nearby hedge to throw against the door to hide it.

Pam got stung again by the nettles, and almost

cried with the pain. Peter had to hunt for dock-leaves again!

" Cheer up! " he said. " What do a few nettle-stings matter? We've had quite an adventure this afternoon! We'll come back here again soon and have a fine time."

Pam wasn't sure she wanted to. But she didn't say so! The boys talked eagerly about the afternoon's excitement on the way home—and by the time they reached the house, Pam had begun to think that nettle-stings or no nettle-stings, it had all been simply marvellous!

CHAPTER 5

IN THE MIDDLE OF THE NIGHT

THE NEXT day Aunt Hetty took Pam and Peter and their cousin Brock in the pony-cart to the sea, which was about three miles away. This was such fun that the three children forgot all about Cliff Castle for a day or two. And then something happened that reminded them of it.

It was something that happened in the middle of the night. Pam woke up and felt very thirsty. She remembered that Aunt Hetty had left a jug of water and a tumbler on the mantelpiece and she got up to get it.

She stood at the window, drinking the water. It

was a moonlit night, but the moon kept going behind clouds. It showed up Cliff Castle very clearly, when it shone down. But when it went behind the clouds the castle was just a black mass on the hill.

Then Pam saw something flickering quickly somewhere at the top of the castle. It caught her eye for a second and then disappeared. What could it be?

She stood watching the castle, forgetting to drink the cool water. Then the flicker came again, this time farther down the castle. Then it disappeared once more. It came for the third and last time at the bottom.

Pam felt excited. She remembered what the woman at the little shop had said about queer lights being seen in the castle. Now here they were again—and they were real, because Pam had seen them!

" I really must wake the boys and tell them! " she thought. " I know it isn't a dream now—but in the morning I might think it was, and not tell them. But it isn't a dream, I've seen the lights! "

She crept down the stairs and into the open door of the boys' room. They were both sleeping peacefully. Pam shook Peter and he woke up with a jump.

" What is it? " he said loudly, sitting up in bed, surprised to see that it was night.

" Sh! " said Pam. " It's me, Peter. Listen—I got up to get a drink of water—and I saw lights in Cliff Castle! "

" Golly! " said Peter, jumping out of bed and going to the window. " Did you really? I say— let's wake Brock."

But Brock was already awake, disturbed by the noise. He was soon told what the matter was, and went to the window, too. All three watched for a little time—and then, suddenly, a light flickered again, this time at the bottom of the castle.

" There it is! " said Pam, clutching Peter and making him jump almost out of his skin. " Did you see it? "

" Of course," said Peter. " And there it is again —on the first floor somewhere this time—and there again, higher up—and now it's right at the very top. Somewhere in that tower, look. It's the very tower we were in the other day! "

Pam felt a bit frightened. Who could be in the castle so late at night? The children watched for a little longer and then went back to bed, puzzled and excited.

" I vote we go there to-morrow again, and see if there's anyone there," said Brock. Nothing ever frightened Brock, and nothing ever stopped him from smiling! He meant to find out the secret of Cliff Castle as soon as possible!

So the next day three excited children met in Brock's play-house in the garden to discuss their plans. They all felt certain that somebody was living in, or visiting, the castle—someone who had no right to be there. Who could it be—and why did he go there?

" When can we go? " asked Peter eagerly.

" After dinner," said Brock. " We're going over to the market this morning, in the next town. We don't want to miss that. It's fun. Dad will take us in his car."

So it was not until after the three children had been to the market, and had come back and eaten a most enormous dinner that they set off to Cliff Castle once again.

They stopped at the little shop where once before they had bought lemonade. The woman served them again with sweet drinks, which they drank in the shop.

" Any more been heard about the lights in Cliff Castle? " they asked the woman, when they paid her. She shook her head.

" Not that I know of," she said. " But don't you go wandering about there, my dears. It's a dangerous place."

They went off again, and soon came near the castle, which towered above them on its hill. They climbed the hill by the narrow rocky path and came to the big flight of overgrown stone steps.

" We won't go up the steps, in case there really is somebody in the castle, watching," said Peter. " We'll try and find that tiny little door. You know—the one we left latched."

So they made their way around nettle patches and other weeds until they came to where the little low door was set in the thick stone walls. The branches they had pulled from the nearby hedge were still against it. Nobody had disturbed them.

They pulled at the door, lifting the iron latch as

they did so. It opened silently, and the children
squeezed through, shutting it after them. They
stood in the big kitchen, so dark and musty, shining
their torches all around.

There was nothing new to be seen. They crossed
the kitchen and went out into the hall—and here
Brock gave a cry of surprise, and levelled his torch
steadily on something on the ground.

The others looked. Pam couldn't make out why
Brock was so excited, because all she saw were
footprints crossing and re-crossing the floor—and,
after all, they had all walked there themselves last
time!

" What's the matter? " she said.

" Can't you see, silly? " said Peter, pointing to a
set of footprints that went across the floor. " Look
at those. Those are not our marks. None of us
have feet as big as that, and certainly we don't
wear boots studded with nails. You can see the
mark the nails have made in the thick dust."

Pam and the others stared at the marks. Yes—
it was quite plain that somebody grown-up had
walked across that floor. Brock found another
track and shone his torch on it.

" *Two* men have been here," he said thoughtfully.
" Look—this set of prints shows a narrower foot
than the other. Now, I wonder whatever two men
were doing here? "

The children stared at one another. They
couldn't imagine why men should visit the castle
in the middle of the night. Perhaps they had come
to steal something?

"Let's look in the rooms down here and see if anything has been disturbed," said Brock at last. So they opened the nearest door and looked into the room there, still festooned with cobwebs, and still smelling the same horrid, musty smell.

"Nothing has been moved," said Brock. "And there are only *our* footprints here. No one else's. Let's follow these other prints and see where they go. They show very clearly, don't they?"

They did show clearly in the thick dust. It was fairly easy to sort them out from the tracks the children themselves had made, for the men's prints were large and had made more impression in the dust. The children followed the prints up the big stairway to the first floor. There, neatly outlined in the dust, was something else!

"Look at that big oblong shape marked in the dust!" said Brock. "It looks as if someone had put down a big box there, doesn't it?"

"Yes," said Peter. "And look—there's the mark of another box, or something, farther along. It looks as if the men had been carrying something very heavy up the stairs, and had put their load down for a rest before going on. See how their footprints are muddled here, too—as if they had picked up their load again and gone on carrying farther along."

"I feel rather like a detective!" said Pam excitedly. "Tracking things like this! I wonder where the men took their loads to! I expect that explains the lights we saw last night. The men had torches, and every time they passed one of those slit-like windows, the reflection shone out for a moment, like a flicker. I guess they didn't know that!"

"Come on," said Brock impatiently. "Let's follow on."

They went on, past many closed doors and up another flight of stone steps. This brought them to the second floor. The footprints still went on!

"I believe they're going up to that tower!" said Pam. "We saw the light flicker there, you know. Oh—I hope the men aren't hiding there!"

This made the boys stop hurriedly. They hadn't thought of that! Suppose somebody was up there in the tower? That wouldn't be very pleasant, because they would be sure to be angry to see children interfering.

"We'd better go very quietly indeed, and not speak a word!" said Brock in a whisper. "Come on."

So in complete silence, their hearts beating fast, the three children crept on and up until they came to the room where the little stone staircase led up into the tower. They mounted it quietly, seeing the men's footprints still on the steps.

They came to the wooden door that had been open the first time they had gone up the staircase. This time it was shut!

CHAPTER 6

A PUZZLE

" It's shut! " whispered Brock. " Shall I try and open it? "

" No! " said Pam.

" Yes! " said Peter. Pam clutched Peter's hand. She didn't know what she expected to find behind that closed door, but she felt certain it wouldn't be nice! The boys felt that they really *must* push the door open. They were bursting with curiosity. Brock pushed. It didn't open. He took hold of the iron handle and tried to turn it. It turned—but still the door didn't open.

" Look through the keyhole and see if you can

see anything," said Peter eagerly. "It's so big that maybe you can."

Brock put his eye to the keyhole. "It's all so dark," he said, "but I believe I can make out shapes of boxes and things. You take a peep, Peter."

So first Peter and then Pam peered through the keyhole, and they both agreed that certainly there were things there that hadn't been there before. They couldn't possibly see if they were boxes or trunks, or what they were, but there *were* things hidden there.

"If only we could get inside and see what's there!" said Brock longingly. "Something that ought not to be there, I'm sure!"

The castle was so silent and lonely, and the sound of their whispering voices was so queer, echoing down the stone stairway, that Pam felt nervous again. She pulled at Peter's arm.

"Let's go," she said. "We'll come back another time. Shall we tell anyone about what we know?"

"I don't think so," said Brock. "It's our own mystery. We've discovered it. Let's try and solve it ourselves. We often read about secrets and mysteries in books—it would be fun to try and keep this one all to ourselves."

They went downstairs again, puzzled to know what was in the tower, and why it was locked. When they got into the hall, Brock switched his torch towards the front door.

"I suppose the men came in at the front," he began—and then, he suddenly stopped. "Look!"

he said, " there are no footsteps leading from the front door. Isn't that queer? How did the men get in, then? "

The three children stared in silence at the enormous door. Certainly the men had not used it. Then which door had they used? As far as the children knew there was only one other door, and that was the little low one they themselves had used. They felt quite certain that the men had not used the window above, where the tree touched, because it was as much as the three children could do to squeeze inside there. No grown-up could possibly manage it.

" Let's follow all the footprints and see where they lead from," said Brock. " If we follow them all, we are sure to come to where the men entered."

So, their torches directed on the ground, the children followed the tracks patiently, one after another. They couldn't understand one lot of tracks at all. They apparently led to, and came from, a room that had once been used as a study. The footprints went in and out of the door—there was a double-track, one going and one coming—and led across the room to the big fireplace, and back again.

" Why did the men come into this room, and out again? " said Pam, puzzled. " They don't seem to have touched anything here. Why did they come here? "

" Goodness knows," said Brock, switching off his torch. " Just idle curiosity, or something, I suppose. There doesn't seem anything for them to

come for, here. I say—look at the time. We shall
be awfully late for tea! "

" We'd better go, then," said Peter, who,
although he wanted his tea, didn't want to leave
the mystery unsolved like that. " Come on.
We'll come back again soon."

They went into the kitchen and out of the little,
low door. They pushed it to behind them, and
piled the boughs against it, dragging the gorse
bush round again. It hid the door well.

" I hope the men aren't as smart as we are! "
said Brock, looking back at the castle. " We've
left plenty of footprints there for them to see. They
could easily tell that three children have been
wandering about."

" I only wish I knew how the men got in and
went out," said Peter, still worrying about that. " I
feel sure there must be something in that room we
last went into to account for their coming and
going."

But it wasn't until late that night, when Peter
was in bed, that he suddenly thought of something
most exciting! Why ever hadn't he thought of it
before? He sat up in bed and called Brock's name
in such an urgent voice that Brock, half-asleep,
woke up in a hurry.

" What's up? " he said. " More lights showing
in Cliff Castle? "

" No," said Peter. " But I believe I know how
the men got in and out, Brock! "

" You don't! " said Brock.

" Well, listen—you know that often there were

secret ways made into and behind rooms through the big chimneys they had in the old days," said Peter. " Well, I believe there must be some kind of way into that room—and that's how the men got into the castle! "

" Crumbs! " said Brock, wide awake now. " I never thought of that. I wonder if you're right. Maybe there's a secret entrance, then! "

" We'll jolly well go to-morrow and find out! " said Peter, " even if we all get as black as sweeps exploring that chimney! What ho for a real adventure to-morrow! "

The two boys told Pam their idea in the morning, and the girl's eyes shone as she listened.

" Gracious! Do you really think there might be a secret way in and out of the castle through that big chimney-place? It's certainly enormous. I looked up it and it would take two or three men easily! "

To their great disappointment the children could not go that day to the castle, because Brock's mother had planned a picnic for them. She was surprised when the three children did not seem pleased about it.

Next day the three children set off once more to the castle. They knew the way very well now and took a few short cuts so that it did not take them very long to arrive at the bottom of the hill. They stared up at the great castle, and it seemed to look down on them with a frown.

" Frown all you like! " said Brock, with a grin. " We'll find out your secret one day! "

They made their way to the little low door they knew and pulled it open. Into the vast kitchen they went, quite silently. Brock switched on his torch to see if there were any more footsteps to be seen. But there were none. In the hall and up the stairs were the same sets of prints that had been there before—there were no new ones, so far as the children could see.

"The men haven't been here again," said Brock. "Come on—let's go into that room where the prints led to and from the fireplace."

So into it they went, and followed the sets of prints to the big, open chimney-place. This was of stone, and the three children could easily stand upright in it!

"Now, we'll just have a hunt and see if, by any chance, there's a way out of the chimney itself," said Brock, and he switched his torch on to examine the stonework.

"Look!" cried Pam, pointing to something that ran up one side of the stone chimney. "A little iron ladder!"

The three of them stared at the little ladder. In the middle of each rung the rust had been worn away a little. "That's where the men went up and down!" cried Brock. "Come on—up we go! We're on to something here!"

CHAPTER 7

A STRANGE PASSAGE

BROCK WENT first up the little iron ladder. Peter followed, and then Pam. The ladder went up some way, and then ended.

"It's come to an end!" cried Brock. "But there's a broad ledge here. I'll give you a hand up, Peter."

He pulled Peter up on to the stone ledge, and then the two boys pulled Pam up beside them. The ledge was broad enough to hold all the children quite comfortably.

"This funny ledge seems to have been made about half-way up the chimney, just before it begins to get very narrow," said Brock, pointing his torch upwards, and showing the others how the chimney suddenly narrowed just above their heads. "We couldn't have gone up much farther, even if there had been a ladder."

"Well, what did the men do?" said Pam, puzzled. "Surely they didn't just come to this ledge and go back?"

"Of course not!" said Brock. "This is where we use our brains a bit. Somewhere round about this ledge is the key to the secret passage that the men used. We've got to find it!"

"You don't mean a real key that turns, do you?" asked Pam, looking round and about with her torch, as if she expected to see a large iron key somewhere.

"Of course not," said Brock impatiently. "I don't exactly know what we're looking for, Pam—maybe a lever—or a handle of some sort—or a stone that moves when it's pushed. We just don't know till we try."

So they tried. They hunted for any small bit of iron that might serve as a handle to move a stone. But they could find nothing in the walls around. They pushed against every stone they could reach, but they all seemed as solid as could be. They knocked with their knuckles to see if any stone sounded hollower than the rest, but except for taking the skin off their knuckles, there was no other result!

It was terribly disappointing. The children looked at one another, after about twenty minutes, and wondered what else to do.

" I'm afraid we're beaten," said Peter, at last.
" There doesn't seem a thing here that might show
us where a secret passage is."

" There's only one place we haven't looked,"
said Pam suddenly.

The boys stared at her. " We've looked simply
everywhere! " said Brock. " You know we have,
silly."

" Well, we haven't looked at the stones we're
standing on! " said Pam. " We've looked at the
stonework around and above us—but not beneath
our feet! "

" Pam's right! " said Brock excitedly. " Good
for you, Pam. You may be only a girl, but you get
the right ideas sometimes! "

Pam felt pleased. She only hoped she was right
in her idea! The three of them knelt down to
examine the stonework under their feet.

It wasn't long before Peter gave a loud cry, which
made the others jump. " Look! What's this in
this stone? "

They all looked closely, shining their torches
down. Set deep in a hole in the rough stone was a
sunken iron handle. On the stone by the handle a
rough arrow was carved, pointing towards the
chimney-hole.

" This is it! " cried Peter. " Brock, what do we
do? Pull at the handle? "

" Wait," said Brock. " This arrow means something. See where it points to? Well, I think we
we have to pull in that direction. Get off the stone,
Pam, and Peter and I will see what we can do."

Pam took her foot off the stone, and watched as the two boys took hold of the iron handle and heaved at it in the direction of the arrow. At first nothing happened at all—and then a very strange thing came to pass under their eyes!

As the boys heaved at the handle, the stone in which it was set began to move smoothly outwards as if it were on rollers! It moved towards the chimney-hole, and then, when it seemed as if it really must overbalance and fall down the chimney, it stopped moving. In the space where it had been was a dark hole that led downwards!

" Look—there's something just a little way down, coiled up on a big staple! " cried Peter, and he shone his torch on it. " It's a rope! "

Brock reached down and pulled it up. It wasn't a rope—it was a rope-ladder. He saw that the top of it was firmly hitched to the staple, and the rest dropped down out of sight. He let go and the rope-ladder swung back to its staple.

" Well, that's the way we go! " said Brock. He shone his torch on to Pam. " What do you feel about it? " he asked. " I know girls aren't so daring as boys. Would you like Peter to take you outside and leave you to wait in the sunshine somewhere, whilst we see where this goes to? It might be a bit dangerous."

" Brock, don't be so mean! " cried Pam indignantly. " I'm not a coward—and do you suppose I want to go away from here just when things are getting really thrilling? I'm coming with you, so that's that."

"Righto," said Brock, grinning. "I thought you would. Don't get all hot and bothered about it. I'll go first. Peter, shine your torch down, old man."

Peter shone his torch down the curious hole, and Brock let himself over the edge and felt about with his feet for the first rung of the rope-ladder. Then down he went, very cautiously. After a bit, he shouted up:

"The ladder has come to an end. There's stone floor here, and a passage leading off. Come on down. Send Pam first, Peter, then you can give her a hand down."

So Pam went next, so thrilled that she could hardly feel for the rungs with her feet! She went down and down, and at last stood beside Brock, her feet safely on solid floor again. Then came Peter. They shone their torches into the passage that led off to the left of the queer hole.

"This is a real secret passage," said Brock in an excited voice. "A really proper one. Golly—isn't it fun!"

"Come on," said Peter. "Let's see where it leads to. I can hardly hold my torch still, my hand is shaking so!"

They went down the narrow winding stone passage. It was perfectly dry, rather airless, and very small. In places, the children had to bend their heads so as not to knock them against the roof of the passage.

The passage went steeply down, then at intervals turned right back on itself. "It must be made in

"*This is a real secret passage,*" said Brock in an excited voice.

the walls of the castle itself," said Brock wonderingly. "What a funny thing for anyone to have thought of making. Hallo—what's this?"

A shaft of daylight had suddenly appeared in one side of the passage! It came from an iron grille set in the wall of the passage itself.

"A sort of air-hole, I suppose," said Peter, and he looked out. "I say, do you know where we are? We are at the west side of the castle—the side that goes sheer down with the steep cliff. I believe there must be a way cut down through the cliff itself, and the entrance to it is somewhere at the bottom of it!"

"Yes—you're right," said Brock, peering out too. "Well, if that's so, the passage will soon change from a stone one to an earth one—and let's hope it hasn't fallen in anywhere."

"Well, the men used it, didn't they?" said Peter.

Just as Brock said, the passage soon changed from a stone-walled one to one whose walls were made of earth, strengthened here and there by wood and stones. It zigzagged down, and at the steepest places steps were cut. It was not an easy way to take.

"We must surely be nearly at the bottom!" said Brock at last. "My legs are getting jolly tired."

There was still a little way to go—and then the secret passage ended abruptly in a small, low cave. The children crept into it, and then out into a larger cave. The entrance to this was set so closely about with gorse and blackberry bushes that it would have been quite impossible to see from the outside.

The children forced their way out, tearing their clothes and scratching their legs.

" You can see where the men got in and out," said Brock. " Just there, where sprays of bramble are broken."

They looked round and about. They were now at the very bottom of the steep side of the cliff, where few people came. It was quite impossible to see the cave from where they stood, although they were only a few feet from it.

" Do you think we'd better climb back and swing that moving stone back into its place? " said Peter suddenly. " If the men come again, as it's pretty certain they will, they'll see that stone is moved, and suspect someone has been after them."

Brock looked at his watch. " We haven't time to do it," he said in dismay. " Golly, Mother will be angry with us—it's half an hour past dinner-time already! "

" But, Brock—suppose the men see the stone is moved? " said Peter anxiously.

" We'll come back another time and put it into its place," said Brock. " Maybe the men won't be back for some time now. They don't come every night. Come on, now—we'll have to *race* back! "

And race back they did—but it didn't prevent them from being well scolded by Brock's mother!

CHAPTER 8

BROCK'S ADVENTURE

THE CHILDREN went to Brock's play-house that afternoon, and talked and talked about their discoveries in the castle. They couldn't say enough about the finding of the strange secret passage. When they remembered that long dark climb downwards through the walls of the castle, and then down the cliff itself, they felt more and more thrilled.

But Peter also went on feeling uncomfortable about the stone in the chimney. He kept saying that the men might come back and discover it.

"Perhaps you're right," said Brock, at last. "I'll slip off this evening, after tea, by myself, and put it back. It won't take me long now I know all the short cuts."

" All right," said Peter. But it was not to be, for Brock's mother wanted him to drive the pony-cart over to the farm and collect a crate of chickens for her.

" Oh, Mother! Won't it do to-morrow? " said Brock in dismay. " I've got something I want to do this evening."

" Well, I'm afraid *that* must keep till to-morrow," said his mother. " I've arranged with the farmer to send over for the chickens this evening and he'll have them all ready. Take Peter and Pam with you. It's a nice drive."

So Brock had to go off with his cousins in the pony-cart. " Just after I'd really made up my mind to go and do that at the castle," he grumbled. " I hate changing my plans. I really do feel you're right about that stone now, Peter."

" So do I," said Peter, gloomily. " It would be just our luck if the men came to-night! "

" I'll tell you what I'll do! " said Brock suddenly. " I'll go as soon as we're in bed! It will just be getting dark then, but the moon will be up early to-night, and I'll be able to see my way back beautifully."

" Oooh, Brock! You surely don't want to go to the castle at night-time! " cried Pam in horror. She felt quite nervous enough in the daytime, and she knew she would never be brave enough to go at night!

" Why not? " said Brock with a laugh. " You

don't think I'm frightened, surely? It would take more than Cliff Castle to make *me* afraid! "

" Shall I come with you? " said Peter. He didn't really want to, but he felt he ought to make the offer.

" No, thanks," said Brock. " I think it would be best for just one of us to go."

All Brock's family were early bedders, and it was about half-past ten when the boy got cautiously out of bed and began to dress himself. Twilight still hung about the fields, but would soon disappear. Then the moon would come up.

" Good luck, Brock! " whispered Peter. " Do you think your father and mother are asleep? "

" I don't know," said Brock. " I'm not going to risk going downstairs and opening any of the doors. They are sure to creak! "

" Well, how are you going, then? " asked Peter in astonishment.

" Down my old apple tree! " whispered Brock, and Peter saw the flash of his white teeth as he grinned.

He went to the window and put a leg across. He caught hold of a strong branch, and in a moment had worked his way down it to the trunk. Then down he slid and Peter heard the soft thud of his feet on the ground below. He watched the boy's shadowy figure as he ran down the garden and out into the lane.

" I hope he won't be too long," thought Peter, as he curled up in bed again. " I shall keep awake till he comes back. Then I'll pop up and wake

Pam, and she can come down and hear what Brock has to say."

But Peter didn't keep awake. By the time that half-past eleven had struck downstairs, he was fast asleep!

But Brock was wide awake, running like a hare over the fields. He met nobody, for no one was out so late at night in the country. Grazing sheep lifted their heads to look at him and a startled rabbit skipped out of his way.

Brock saw the moon coming up slowly. It lighted up the castle on the hill, and made it look silvery and unreal.

" It's like a castle out of some old story," thought the boy. " It will be fun to get inside at night-time! "

Brock was quite fearless. He enjoyed this kind of adventure, and was quite glad to be on his own, without the others to bother about. He ran round to where the little low door was set at the bottom of the castle. He pulled at it and it opened.

He slipped inside. He waited a moment in the great dark kitchen to see if anyone else was about by any chance, but everything was still and silent. The boy switched his torch on, and went into the hall to see if there were any more footprints. But there were none. So the men hadn't yet been— but, after all, it wasn't many hours since Brock had left, and it didn't leave much time for anyone to come.

The boy made his way to the room where the iron ladder led up the chimney. He climbed up the ladder, and soon came to the ledge. The stone that had moved out to disclose the secret passage was still swung out over the chimney-hole. Brock wondered how to get it back.

" I suppose I must heave on the iron handle in the opposite direction," he thought. He took hold of it—and then almost fell down the hole in astonishment. He had heard voices!

" Golly! " thought the boy, sitting quite still on the ledge, " somebody is coming—two people at least. But where do the voices come from? "

Brock couldn't distinguish any words, he could only hear the murmur of voices, talking and answering. They came up from the hole, and were getting louder.

" My goodness, someone is coming up through the secret passage! " thought the boy, in a fright for the moment. " It must be those men. I must get the stone back into place as quickly as I can! "

With the sound of voices, came other sounds rather like something being bumped against the wall. Brock felt sure the men were carrying something again. He took hold of the iron handle sunk in the stone and heaved hard at it. At first the stone would not move—then, slowly and gradually, it gave way to Brock's stout pulling, and rolled back into its place.

It made a slight grinding noise as it did so, and Brock hoped that the men below were talking loudly enough to drown the sound. He climbed quickly down the iron ladder and ran into the kitchen, meaning to get out of the little low door.

Then he stopped. "No," he said to himself. "This is a big chance for me to find out exactly what the men are up to. I'll hide somewhere, and listen and follow. Golly, what an adventure!"

He darted behind a big cupboard in the hall, and waited to see what happened. After some while he heard sounds coming from the room he had left. The men were climbing down the iron ladder in the chimney-place, dragging something heavy with them.

Then came the sound of voices, quite clearly, echoing weirdly through the silent castle.

"We ought to be paid double for bringing the goods up that narrow way!" grumbled one voice. "I'd be willing to risk the front door, but Galli won't hear of it. Come on—we've got to take the things up to the tower now. Then we'll get away quickly. I don't like this wretched moon, showing us up so clearly when we walk outside."

From his hiding-place Brock could see two men, each carrying large and heavy boxes on their shoulders. They were half-bent beneath the weight, and the boy marvelled that they could possibly have carried them all the way up the secret passage, up the rope ladder, and then down the iron one!

"They must be very strong," thought the boy. They were. They had broad shoulders, and when they were caught in a shaft of bright moonlight, Brock saw that they looked rather foreign. He had thought that their voices sounded a little foreign, too. They were very dark and swarthy, and one man wore gold ear-rings in his ears.

They came into the hall, carrying the boxes, and then went up the broad flight of stairs. They put the boxes down for a rest when they came to the top, and again Brock heard the murmur of their voices as they spoke together. The boy crept out from his hiding-place and went to the foot of the stairs.

He followed the men silently up and up until they went into the room from which the little stone staircase led into the tower-room. One of the men unlocked the door at the top. Brock heard them put down their loads and sigh with relief.

" I could do with a drink now," said one man. " Is there a well in the kitchen—or somewhere we can get water? "

" We'll look," said the other. He locked the door, and the men came down the narrow staircase again. Brock saw that they had left the key in the door and his eyes gleamed. Maybe he could slip up and take it out before they remembered it—and then he and the others could come and find out what was in those boxes! Something exciting, he was sure!

He slipped out before the men, and ran into one of the nearby rooms. It was furnished, and the boy pulled some curtains around him to hide himself. But the things were quite rotten and fell away as he touched them. Thin grey dust flew all around, and before Brock could stop himself, he sneezed!

CHAPTER 9

BROCK IN TROUBLE

Now WHEN Brock sneezed, everyone knew it, for he sneezed heartily and well. In the silence of the castle his sneeze made a most tremendous noise! It echoed all round and about, and startled poor Brock just as much as it startled the two men.

"There's someone here!" said one. "In that room. Quick—we'll get him!"

They darted into the room where Brock had tried to hide. Luckily for him they missed him and he was able to dart out and elude their outstretched hands. He ran down the stairs at top speed, his boots making tremendous clatter as he went.

The men ran after him. Down and down went Brock, meaning to make for the little low door in the kitchen. But when he got there, it was so dark he could not see where he was going, and he fell over a stool. He crashed to the floor, and had no time to make for the door. Instead, he rolled quickly under a big oak-seat in the fireplace and lay there, hardly daring to breathe. The men switched on their torches, and one of them gave an exclamation.

" Look here—here's a little door, ajar! "

" That's where the boy came in! " said the other man. " Well, he didn't have time to get out, that's certain. He's somewhere here. But first I think we'll shut and lock the door. Then our friend won't be able to escape quite so easily as he hoped! "

Poor Brock heard the door being shut and locked. He felt certain that the man had put the key in his pocket. He couldn't think what to do. He wondered if the men knew of the little back stair-case. If he could run up that he might be able to find the room where the big tree touched the window-sill. Then he'd be out in a jiffy and the men couldn't follow him!

" Let's shut the kitchen door, and have a good hunt round," said one man. " He's here some-where."

Now was Brock's chance. The big kitchen door was at the far end of the kitchen. He stood up quietly, and then made a dash for the little back staircase, which was quite nearby. The men gave a shout when they heard him, and switched their torches round to the noise.

"There's a stairway there!" cried one. "He's gone up. Come on—after him!"

The men tore up the narrow stairway after Brock. "If only I could remember which room that tree touched!" thought the boy desperately. "But we couldn't find it again before. There are so many rooms here, all exactly the same!"

He ran on till he came to a room and then he darted inside. He took off his boots quickly, because he knew that the noise they made gave him away and made him easy to follow.

The men passed the room, flashing their torches ahead of them. Brock ran to the window. Alas, it was not the right one. It was far too narrow to squeeze out.

Brock ran to the door and peered out. The men had gone to the other end of the stone landing and were looking into each of the rooms as they came back. Brock ran into the one next to his. Again he was disappointed. It was not the right one. He went into a third, his heart beating fast, for the men were now coming back. But again he was unlucky.

He did not dare to go into another room. The only thing he could do was to run back to the staircase and go down it, hoping to hide himself so well somewhere that he would not be found.

As he ran to the staircase the men saw him in a shaft of moonlight and raced after him. Brock almost fell down the stairs, and raced across the kitchen into the hall. Then he tore into one of the big, furnished rooms, meaning to hide behind some furniture.

The men saw him. They went into the room after him, and in a few moments they had found Brock and dragged him out from behind a big dusty couch that smelt so mouldy that the boy was almost sick.

" Well, we've got you now! " said the man. He shone his torch into Brock's face. " What are you doing here, spying on us? You're doing a dangerous thing. We can't let you go, because you've found our secret, and we daren't risk your telling it till we've finished our job and are safe."

Brock said nothing. His red, round face looked surly. The men looked at one another.

" What are we to do with him? " said one. " He's only a kid. We'd better lock him up somewhere and tell Galli. Then he can put him away till it's safe to let him go. Well, youngster, you'll be sorry for yourself when Galli gets hold of you. He won't be gentle with a nastly little boy who spies on him! "

Still Brock said nothing. One of the men gave him a shake. " He's lost his tongue," he said to the other. " Come on—let's lock him up in the tower-room with the boxes. He'll be safe there."

So Brock was dragged up to the tower-room, and put there among the big boxes. The men locked the door behind them, and Brock heard their footsteps going down the stairs. He felt sure they would go out by the little low door instead of the difficult way down the secret passage. And they would lock the door behind them, so that Peter and Pam couldn't get in if they came to look for him.

" I've made a mess of things," said Brock, looking at the big boxes. " I wonder what's in those boxes. How I'd like to know! "

He shone his torch on to one, but soon saw that it was so well fastened and nailed down that it would need strong tools to open it. His bare hands and pocket-knife would be no good at all! He went to a window and looked out gloomily on the countryside. A ray of moonlight came through the slit. Far away, Brock could see his own house.

As he looked at it, he saw a light moving in one of the windows. He tried to reckon out which it was, and soon came to the conclusion that it was his own window. Then Peter must be awake. That must have been his torch shining!

In a trice Brock took out his own torch again, and pushed it as far as he could through the slit. He pressed the knob of the torch up and down, up and down, so that it flashed regularly and continually.

" If only Peter sees, it, he may guess it's me," thought the boy. " Oh, I do hope he sees it! I don't want to be kept a prisoner here for days! "

CHAPTER 10

PETER AND PAM TO THE RESCUE!

PETER SLEPT soundly till half-past one. Then he woke up with a jump. He remembered at once that Brock had gone to Cliff Castle, and he sat up in bed to see if the boy was back.

He stared at Brock's empty bed, and then switched on his torch to look at his watch. Half-past one! Whatever could Brock be doing?

As he sat wondering, he heard a sound at the door, and almost jumped out of his skin as a white figure came into the room. It was Pam in her night-dress.

" Peter! Is Brock back? You said you'd come

up and wake me when he came back, but it's awfully late."

Peter shone his torch on to Brock's empty bed. Pam felt scared.

" Golly! Where is he? " She went to the window and stared out at the big black mass of Cliff Castle. The moon had gone in for a moment, and it looked very dark and forbidding. Then she suddenly caught sight of a bright little light winking and blinking in the top tower to the right.

" That's funny," she said to Peter. " Look at that light, flashing every other moment, Peter, just as if it were a signal. Those men wouldn't do that, would they, because they wouldn't want to give themselves away. But who else would be signalling like that? "

Peter looked, and as soon as he saw the winking light he guessed that it was Brock. " It's old Brock! " he said. " I'm quite sure it is! What's he doing in the tower-room—it was locked, wasn't it? He must have got in somehow and wants us to go and see what the treasure is in those boxes! "

" Or do you think he's been captured? " said Pam slowly. " He might have been, you know. Maybe he's locked up in the tower."

" We'd better go and see," said Peter, beginning to dress hurriedly. " We won't tell Aunt Hetty, or Uncle, Pam, in case Brock wants us to go and see the treasure with him without anyone knowing. We don't want to give the secret away unless we have to! Hurry and dress now! "

It wasn't long before the two children were

climbing down the old apple tree and sliding to the ground below. Then they made their way to Cliff Castle, panting as they ran.

They got there safely, and went to where the little, low door was set in the kitchen wall. Peter pulled at it, expecting it to open. But it didn't. It remained tightly shut.

"I say! It's locked or something!" he said to Pam. "Here, help me to pull."

But pulling was no use at all. The little wooden door wouldn't budge!

"Well, Brock wouldn't have locked it, that's certain," said Peter, speaking in a whisper. "Some-one else must have. I say—I rather think old Brock's been captured!"

"How shall we get in, then?" she whispered. "Up that tree? But, Peter, surely we can't climb it in the dark."

"We'll have to try," said Peter. "Look, the moon will be out for some time now—we'll climb whilst it gives us a bright light. I'll help you. Or would you rather stay on the ground whilst I climb?"

"No, I'll climb, too," said Pam bravely. So they made their way to the tree and Peter shinned up it first. But Pam couldn't climb it because her legs trembled so. "I'll just have to stay here," she whispered up to him. "I shall fall if I climb up, Peter. Isn't it sickening?"

"Never mind, old girl," said Peter. "You stay down below and warn me if anyone comes. I'll go in and see if I can rescue Brock."

Pam couldn't see Peter climbing the tree because it was full of dark shadows, flecked by moonlight. She heard the rustling, though, and knew when Peter had reached the bough that led to the window because of the sudden swinging of the tree.

Peter didn't find it so easy to climb the tree in the dark as in the light, but he managed to slide down the branch to the window, and then squeezed himself through. He jumped down on the floor. His boots made a noise, and he took them off. He ran on tiptoe to the door, not making a sound. When he got there he looked out, and suddenly remembered how hard it had been to find that room again. He took one of his boots and made a big cross with it in the dust of the floor. Now he had only to pop his head in at the door to see the cross and know it was the room with the tree outside.

" I feel quite clever! " said the boy to himself. He ran to the little stone staircase and went lightly down it. The moon was now high and shone in at every slit-like window, so that it was fairly easy to see, though the shadows were as black as could be.

Across the kitchen went the boy, and into the dark hall. Then up the broad flight of stairs on the other side, and on to the first landing. He paused there in the shadows to listen. Was there anyone about? After all, if Brock had been captured, someone must have captured him—and it was quite likely they might still be somewhere in the castle. This was rather a weird thought, and the boy felt a shiver down his back.

" I won't get into a fright! " he thought to himself. " I'm rescuing Brock, and I'm not afraid of anything."

He would have liked to whistle to keep his spirits up, but he didn't dare to. As it was, every little sound he made went echoing round and round, and made him jump.

He went on up to the floor where the room was that had the tower staircase leading from it. He came to the stairway, and stood at the bottom, his heart beating so loudly that he felt sure anyone nearby could hear it!

He stole up the staircase, and felt the shut door. He longed to push it open, but he still didn't know if Brock were behind it, or an enemy. And then, suddenly, he knew!

There came the sound of a sigh, and then a creak as if someone had sat down on a box. " Blow my torch! " said a gloomy voice. " It's no use now— the battery's given out. I can't signal any more."

It was Brock's voice. In delight Peter banged on the door, making poor Brock inside almost jump out of his skin, for he had, of course, no idea at all that Peter was anywhere near. He almost fell off the box.

" Brock! " came Peter's voice. " I'm here. I'm coming. What's happened? "

Peter pushed at the door—but alas, it was locked, and wouldn't open. Brock's voice came in excitement from behind the door:

" Peter! You old brick! Is the key in the lock? "

" No," said Peter, switching on his torch. " What a blow! I can't get in—and you can't get out."

Brock told him shortly how he had been captured. " And now I'm sitting on a box that may contain half the jewels in the kingdom! " he said. " But I'm a prisoner, and likely to remain one till this man Galli they keep talking about comes along and decides what's to be done with me."

" I'll go back home and get your father to come, and the police," said Peter eagerly. " I don't expect the men will be back to-night."

" Where's Pam? " said Brock. " Fast asleep in bed, I hope! "

" No. She's outside the castle, waiting," said Peter. " She couldn't climb the tree in the dark. She said she'd keep watch in case someone came."

" I say, Peter! I've got an idea! " said Brock suddenly. " Maybe the other towers have little rooms inside them, with a door like this one. And maybe they all have locks and keys that are the same. Do you think you could go to the tower on this side and see if there's a key in the door of the room there? If there is, bring it back and try it in this lock—it may fit—and open the door! "

" Golly! That's an idea! " cried Peter, and he went down the staircase and made his way round the big stone landing until he came to the end. He went into the room there and found a staircase leading up to the tower above, exactly like the one in the room he had left. Up he went and came to a door.

" And, my goodness, there *is* a key in the lock! "
said the boy to himself, in delight. He pulled out
the key and made his way back. He fitted it into
the lock of Brock's door—and it turned! The lock
gave, and the door opened.

" Oh, Peter—what luck! " said Brock, and he
squeezed his cousin's arm. " Thanks, old man—
you're a brick to rescue me. Now we must go
straight down and join Pam—and then I think we
ought to rush home and wake up my father. Someone ought to come and see what's in these boxes! "

Down the little stone staircase went the two
boys, both in their stockinged feet. They felt
tremendously excited, and Peter's hand shook as
he held out his torch to show the way. The mystery
of Cliff Castle was nearly solved. The secret was in
those boxes. Soon Brock's father would come along
and open them. Then, maybe, the two men would
be caught and everything would be cleared up.

Just as they reached the first landing they had a
terrific shock. A great crashing echoed throughout
the whole castle, and the two boys jumped so much
that they had to stand still. What in the world
could the noise be?

CHAPTER 11

MORE AND MORE EXCITEMENT

THE ENORMOUS crash came again—and then the boys knew what it was!

" It's somebody banging on that great front-door knocker! " cried Peter.

" But who would do that in the middle of the night? " said Brock, amazed.

" Pam, of course, " said Peter proudly. " She said she'd watch out—and I expect she's seen someone coming and that's her way of warning us. What a marvellous idea! "

" I say—what a girl she is! " said Brock admiringly. " Well—we'll have to look out. Let's slip down to the kitchen and see if we can get out of that little low door. Maybe the key is on this side."

They ran quietly down the stairs in their stock-inged feet—and then paused in horror. In the kitchen, waiting silently, themselves amazed at the noise on the front door, were three men. Two of them Brock had seen before.

The men saw the boys and gave a shout. " Two kids this time! " cried one. " Quick, get them! "

The boys tore into the hall and into the big room where the chimney was that gave on to the secret passage. Brock slammed the door and turned the key in the lock. Then they rushed to the fire-place and climbed quickly up the iron ladder. A heave at the iron ring and the stone moved silently across, showing the way down.

A great noise at the locked door made the boys hurry more than ever. The door would certainly be down very soon, for the lock was sure to be rotten!

It was! It gave way and the door swung open. The three men rushed in and paused. " Surely those kids don't know the secret passage! " cried one of the men in amazement.

" They do! " said another. " Come on—we must get them, somehow, or they'll be away, and tell the police."

They rushed to the fireplace and swarmed up the iron ladder. By this time the boys were at the bottom of the rope ladder, making their way as quickly as they could down the secret stone passage, their hearts beating painfully.

They could hear the men coming after them, and hurried more and more. They came to where the stone passage ended and the earth passage began.

"Hurry, Brock, hurry!" cried Peter. "They are almost on us. Hurry!"

Brock did hurry, but the ground was painful to his stockinged feet. At last the boys came to the small cave and made their way into the larger one. Just as the men got to the small cave the boys forced their way out of the large one, and found themselves on the hillside.

"Up a tree, quick!" whispered Brock. "It's our only chance!"

Peter shinned up a nearby tree, with Brock helping him. Then Brock swung himself up into the dark shadows and both boys lay flat on branches, peering down below, hardly daring to breathe.

It didn't occur to the men that the boys could so quickly have gone up a tree. They thought they had run off into the bushes, and they beat about quickly to find them.

"They'll give it up soon," whispered Brock. He was right. The men soon gave up the search and gathered together. The third man, called Galli, was very angry.

"Fancy letting a couple of kids beat you like this!" he said in disgust. "Now there's only one thing to do—get the stuff out of the tower-room at once and find a new hiding-place. Go on—get back to the castle and haul the stuff out."

The men went off, the other two muttering

angrily to themselves, but they were evidently terrified of Galli, who was the leader.

The men went back up the secret passage. As soon as they were safely out of hearing, the boys slid down the tree into the moonlight and looked at one another excitedly.

" Let's get back home as quickly as we can! " said Peter. " We'll fetch Pam, and run as fast as possible."

" The men will be gone by the time we get Dad and the police here," panted Brock, as they ran up the slope that led to the front of the castle, to find Pam. She saw them coming and jumped out from under a bush.

" Brock! Peter! Oh, how glad I am to see you! Did you hear me crash on the knocker? I saw the three men coming, and they went in at that little low door. I couldn't *think* how to warn you—and I suddenly thought of that great knocker! "

" Pam, you're a marvellous girl! " said Brock, and he threw his arm round his cousin's shoulders and gave her a hug. " Nobody but you would have thought of such an idea! Honestly, I'm proud of you! "

The boys quickly told Pam what had happened to them—and then Brock suddenly fell silent. The other two looked at him.

" What is it, Brock? " asked Peter.

" I've got an idea, but I don't know if it's good or not," said Brock. " Listen—those men are all going back to the tower-room, aren't they? Well, do you suppose—do you *possibly* suppose we could get there, too, and wait till they're inside—and then lock them in? "

Peter and Pam stared at Brock. It seemed a mad idea—and yet—suppose, just suppose it could be done!

" The men would never, never guess we were back again," said Peter slowly. " They wouldn't be on the look-out for us. They think we're running off to tell the police. It seems to me that your idea is the only one that might possibly lead to the capture of the men—and the goods, too! Otherwise, by the time we get back here with help, they'll be gone with everything! "

" We'll try it! " said Brock. " Now, look here, Pam—your part in this is to race off by yourself over the fields and wake Daddy and Mother, and tell them everything. Will you do that? "

Pam didn't at all want to do anything of the sort, but she wasn't going to let the boys down. She nodded her head. " I'll go," she said, and she went, running like a little black shadow down the hillside.

" She's a good kid," said Brock, and the two boys turned to go to the castle. They meant to climb up the tree and get in that way. They were sure the little low door would be locked. Up they went and into the dark room. There, on the floor, was the cross in the dust that Peter had made!

" Now, quietly! " whispered Brock, as they went down the narrow stone staircase. " The men may be in the kitchen, or the hall."

The boys stole carefully down. There was no

one in the kitchen—and no one in the hall. The boys kept to the shadows as they walked.

Suddenly they heard a noise, and Peter clutched Brock by the arm, pulling him into the shadow of a great hall curtain. " It's the men coming out of the chimney-place," whispered the boy. " They're only just back. It's taken them ages to come up by that steep secret passage. Keep quiet now. We may be able to do something."

The men clattered across the room to the door and then went across the hall to the big staircase, talking in loud voices. It was quite clear that they had no idea at all that the boys were hidden near-by. They went up the stairs, and as soon as they had turned a corner, the boys followed them, so full of excitement that they could hardly breathe!

The three men went on up to the tower-room. The boys could hear their voices all the time. They crept after them in their stockinged feet. They had never felt so terribly excited in their lives!

All the men went into the tower-room. Peter and Brock stood at the bottom of the little staircase that wound up to the room, and wondered if this was the right moment to go up.

" Better do it now," said Brock, " or they will start to come out again."

Galli, up above, gave orders to the two men. " Take that box first. And hurry up about it! "

There came the sounds of two men swinging a box round to get hold of it.

" *Now!* " whispered Brock, and the two boys shot up the stairs, one behind the other, breathing fast. They got to the door. The men hadn't heard a sound. By the light of their torches Brock could see two of them lifting one of the boxes, whilst Galli stood by. The boy caught hold of the wooden door, and closed it as quietly as he could. But it made a slight click as the latch went into place. At once Galli noticed it and roared out a warning.

" Look out! There's somebody on the stairs! " He rushed to the door. But Brock had already turned the key in the lock.

Galli hammered on the door in a rage and the stout door shook under his blows.

" Hammer all you like! " shouted Brock, exultingly. " You're caught! "

The boys turned to go down the stairs—and then Peter's sharp ears caught something that one of the men said.

" I've got a key to this door! I took it out of the lock when I shut up that kid. Here, take it, Galli, and undo the door. We'll catch those boys if we have to hunt the castle from top to bottom! "

Peter clutched Brock by the arm. " Did you hear that? They've got the key to this door, Brock! The one that was in the door when they locked you up! Now what are we to do? "

Brock dashed up the stairs again. He switched his torch on to the door, at the same moment as he heard a key being put into the lock from the other side. His torch showed him a big bolt at the top of the door and another at the bottom. Hoping and praying that they would not be too rusty to push into place, the boy took hold of the bottom bolt. He pulled at it, but it stuck badly.

Meantime the men on the other side of the door were trying to turn the key to unlock it. But it was more difficult to do that from inside than outside. Muttering a string of foreign-sounding words, Galli tried to force the key round.

" Let me try the bolt, Brock," whispered Peter, and took Brock's place. But it was no use. He could only move it a little way, it was so rusty.

" Try the top one," said Brock. So Peter stood on tiptoe and tried the one at the top. He was trembling from head to foot, for it was terrible to hear someone doing his best to unlock the door from the inside, whilst he, Peter, was trying with all his might to bolt it from the outside!

" Oh Peter, Peter, won't it move? " groaned Brock, feeling certain that they would be captured if the door was unlocked. Peter suddenly gave a shout, and there was a creaking sound. The rust on the bolt had given way and the bolt had slid slowly into place. The door was bolted!

Almost at the same moment the key turned on the other side and unlocked the door—but it was held by the bolt, and Galli roared with rage as he found that the door would not budge. It gave at the bottom, but the stout bolt at the top held firmly.

The boys were both shaking. They had to sit down on the stairs and lean against one another. Neither boy could have gone down the stairs at that moment. They sat there, close to each other, and heard the three men losing their tempers with one another. They shouted in a strange language, and at times one of them would shake the door with all his strength.

" I hope that top bolt holds," said Peter in a whisper. " Everything in this house is so rotten and old that I wouldn't be surprised if the wretched thing gives way."

" Well, let's try to use the bottom bolt as well then, when the men leave the door alone for a moment," whispered back Brock. " Come on—there's a chance now."

The boys, both together, tried to move the bottom bolt back into place. Peter took Brock's knife and scraped away the rust as best he could. Then they tried again—and to their great joy and relief, the bolt slowly and haltingly slipped into place. Now the door was held at top and bottom, and the boys felt pretty certain that the men could not possibly get out, even if they tried all their strength together on the door.

The men did try once more—and this time they found, of course, that it would not move at the bottom.

" They've fastened the door at the bottom, too, now! " shouted Galli, and the angry man struck the door with his fists, and kicked at it viciously with his foot.

" Hope he hurts himself! " whispered Brock, who was feeling much better now. He had stopped shaking, and was grinning to himself to think how neatly all the men were boxed up together. " I say, Peter—I rather think we've done a good night's work! "

" I rather think we have, too! " said Peter, and the two boys hugged themselves as they thought of all they had gone through to catch the men.

" I hope Pam gets home safely," said Brock. " I wonder how long it will be before she brings help back. Some time, I expect, because Dad will have to get in touch with the police. Well—I'm quite content to wait here till somebody arrives. I guess we're feeling a bit more comfortable than those three men! "

CHAPTER 12

THE SECRET COMES OUT!

MEANTIME PAM was speeding across the fields and along the shadowy lanes. Once she had started she no longer felt afraid. She had to bring help to the boys, and that help rested on her swift feet. " Quick, quick! " she kept saying. " I must run like the wind! "

And run like the wind she did. She came to her aunt's house at last, and hammered on the front door, for she did not want to waste time by climbing in at the window. Her uncle awoke at once and came to his window. When he saw Pam standing there in the moonlight he thought he must be dreaming.

"Uncle! Uncle! Let me in, quick!" cried Pam. "There isn't a moment to be lost! The boys are in danger!"

In two minutes Pam was inside the house, sitting on her uncle's knee, pouring out the whole story to him as quickly as she could. He and his wife listened in the utmost amazement. Aunt Hetty could hardly believe the story, but Pam's uncle did at once, and saw that he must act quickly.

"I'll hear all the rest later," he said to the excited little girl. "If those two boys have managed to capture the men as they planned, we must go there at once—and if they haven't managed to, they'll be in the gravest danger. I'll ring up the police now. Hetty, see to Pam. She'd better go back to bed."

But nothing in the world would have persuaded Pam to go back to bed that night! "I'll climb out of the window if you make me go to bed!" she cried. "Oh, Aunt Hetty, I *must* go back to Cliff Castle. I must, I must!"

And, as it turned out, she did, because when her uncle came back from the telephone he said that the police wanted her to go with them to take them to the right room. It wasn't long before a police car roared up to the house with four stout policemen inside!

Pam and her uncle squeezed into the car too, and they set off to Cliff Castle by the road. It was a much longer way than across the fields, but it didn't take very long in the powerful police car.

"Why, look at that light in the sky!" said Pam

suddenly, pointing to the east. " What is it, Uncle? "

" It's the dawn coming! " said her uncle, with a laugh. " The night is going. Hasn't it been a long enough night for you, Pam? "

" Yes, it has," said Pam, suddenly feeling glad that the daylight would soon be there. " I wonder how we can get into the castle, Uncle? There are four ways in—but three of them are almost impossible."

" What are the four ways, Missy? " asked the inspector, who was sitting beside her.

" There's the front door," said Pam, " but the locks and bolts are all rusted, and we couldn't open it. Then there's a little low door set in the foot of the castle by the kitchen—but that's shut and locked. And there's a secret passage from the bottom of the steep cliff, through the walls of the castle, and up a chimney."

" My word! " said the inspector, startled. " However did you find out all this? I must say you children are pretty daring! What's the fourth way in? "

" It's the way we used first," said Pam. " Up a tree and in at a window. But I'm afraid you're all too big to squeeze in there! "

" We'll break in at the little low door! " said the inspector with a chuckle. And that is exactly what they did do!

The two boys were still sitting together on the stairs, feeling rather sleepy, watching the dawn put silver fingers in at the slits of window, when they suddenly heard the noise of the police car roaring up to the castle. Then they heard loud blows on the little door far below.

" They're breaking in! " cried Brock, in excitement, and he jumped to his feet, almost falling down the stairway. " They're knocking down that little door. Now they're in—golly, they're here! Pam! Pam! Here we are! "

Pam came tearing up the big staircase, followed by her uncle and the four policemen. She rushed into the room off which the little winding stairway led up to the tower-room, shouting as she came.

" Peter! Brock! Did you manage to catch the men? Uncle's here and four policemen! "

" Yes, we've got the men! " shouted Brock, and grinned as he saw Pam's excited face coming round a bend in the stairway. " We've bolted them in well and truly! "

The men had fallen silent when they heard the shouts. They knew perfectly well that everything was up, as far as they were concerned.

" Get away down the stairs, you three children," commanded the inspector, suddenly taking on a new and quite stern voice. The children badly wanted to be in at the finish—but they didn't dare to say a word. They had to go and wait in the room below whilst the police unbolted the door and rushed the three men.

There was a lot of yelling and struggling, but the five men against the three were too strong, and it wasn't long before a sorry procession came down the winding stairway in the charge of three policemen.

"Take them into a room and stay with them till I come," ordered the inspector. Then he beckoned to the three children.

"Come along," he said, "we're going to open those boxes. You deserve to see what's inside, since it was you who really captured the men!"

In the greatest excitement, the children followed the inspector and Brock's father upstairs into the tower-room. The great boxes lay there, still unopened.

The inspector had the right tools with him and began to force open the boxes quickly. They were very well fastened indeed, and even when the clasps had been forced back, the ropes cut, and the iron bands severed, there were still the locks to open. But the inspector had marvellous keys for these. "One of these keys will open the locks," he told the watching children. "It's my boast that I've got keys to open any lock in the world!"

The locks of the first box clicked. The inspector threw back the heavy lid. What looked like cotton-wool lay on the top. Pam pulled it aside.

Then everyone cried out in astonishment and awe—for lying in the box were the most marvellous jewels that the children had ever seen or heard of. Great red rubies shone and glowed in necklaces and tiaras. Brilliant green emeralds winked, and diamonds blazed in the light of the torches that shone down on the jewels.

"I say!" said Brock's father, finding his tongue

first. " I say—inspector, these are not ordinary jewels. They are worth a fortune—many fortunes! What are they? "

" Well, it looks to me as if they are the private jewellery of the Princess of Larreeanah," said the inspector. " They were stolen on the steamer, when she fled from her palace in India to this country. It's an amazing story. She had them all put into these boxes and safely fastened in many ways. They were put into the stronghold of the steamer she took. They were apparently guarded night and day—and were taken ashore with her when she landed in this country. But when the boxes were opened at her bank in London, they contained nothing but stones! "

" But how could that be? " said Pam, her eyes opening wide in amazement. " And how are they here, then? "

" Well, I suppose what happened was that one of the guards on the steamer was bribed by some clever thief who knew what was contained in the boxes," said the inspector. " He must have had boxes of exactly the same size and make all ready, filled with stones—probably hidden inside big trunks of his own. At the right moment he must have got into the place where these boxes were stored, exchanged them, and then put these boxes into his own big trunks, and gone ashore safely with them."

" And the poor Princess went off with the boxes of stones! " cried Brock. " Was it that man Galli, do you think? "

"Yes, I should think so," said the inspector, beginning to open another box. "He's very like a famous thief, one of the cleverest we have ever come up against, whom we already want for another daring robbery. He's shaved off his moustache and beard, but I noticed that he had a little finger missing—and so has this thief I was telling you about! My word—look at this!"

The second box was now open, and contained just as amazing treasures as the first. Pam took out a wonderful tiara, rather like a small crown, and put it on.

"Now you're worth about fifty thousand pounds!" said her uncle. "Do you feel grand and important?"

"Oh, very!" said Pam, with a laugh.

"Well, you've every right to feel like that," said the inspector, shutting the first box and locking it. "But not because you're wearing famous jewels. You can feel grand and important because you and your brother and cousin have made it possible for us to recover all this jewellery and to catch the thieves who stole it! At the moment I should say you are the most daring and clever children in the whole of the kingdom!"

Even Brock blushed at this. All the children felt pleased.

"Well, it didn't seem very clever or daring whilst we were doing it," said Peter honestly. "As a matter of fact, I kept feeling frightened—and I know poor old Pam did."

"It's braver to do a thing if you feel afraid than

it is to do it if you don't mind," said the inspector.
" I don't know what to do with these boxes. I
think I'll handcuff those three men together, send
them off in charge of two of my men, and leave
the third man here on guard whilst I go and report
to Scotland Yard."

" What's Scotland Yard? " said Pam in surprise.

" It's the place where all the head-policemen
work! " said the inspector, with a sudden grin.
" Very important place, too! Well—come along.
You children must be tired out."

They went down the stairs. The inspector gave
his orders, and the three sullen thieves were hand-
cuffed together, so that two policemen could easily
take charge of them. The third one was sent up to
guard the tower-room.

" I'll send back a car for Galli and the others,"
said the inspector. " I'll take these children home,
and then their uncle can come along with me to the
station."

Pam almost fell asleep in the car. She was
completely tired out. But the two boys were still
excited. They looked out of the car windows at
the sun just rising in the eastern sky. It seemed ages
and ages since yesterday! Could so much have
possibly happened in one night?

Brock's mother made all the children go to bed
when they got back. " You look absolutely worn
out," she said. " Tell me everything when you
wake, Pam. I'll undress you. You are falling asleep
as you stand! "

The boys were glad to get into bed now, though

it seemed odd to go to bed when the sun was just rising. Brock snuggled down.

" Well, good night," he said to Peter. " I mean, good morning! What adventures we've had. I'm sorry they're over. I did enjoy solving the mystery of Cliff Castle."

" Yes, we soon found out the secret," said Peter. " But, oh—I'm sorry it's all ended! "

But it hadn't quite ended! The Princess of Larreeanah was so overjoyed at the recovery of her jewels that she came herself to see the three adventurous children.

She arrived in a magnificent car, and was wearing some of the jewels. Much to the children's embarrassment, she kissed them all!

They didn't like being kissed by strangers, even if this stranger was a Princess—and they made up their minds they weren't going to like her. But they soon changed that idea when they found what she had brought for them in a small van that followed her car!

" Open the door of the van and see what is inside for you! " she said to the three surprised children. Brock pulled open the doors at the back of the van—and all three stared in amazement and awe at the Princess's wonderful present.

" It's a car—a small car just big enough to take the three of us! " said Brock, staring at the marvellous little car inside the van. It was bright red, with yellow bands and yellow spokes to the wheels. The lamps, wind-screen, and handles shone like silver.

" It goes by electricity," said the Princess. " I had it made especially for you. You don't have to have a driving-licence, of course, because it is listed as a toy car. But actually it is driven just like a real one, has a horn and everything, and goes by electricity, so that you don't need petrol."

" Let's go for a ride in it now! " shouted Peter in excitement. So they pulled out the magnificent little car and got into it. Brock drove it. He pulled a lever, took hold of the steering-wheel, and off went the car down the lane with its three excited passengers.

" What a wonderful end to an adventure! " cried Peter. " Didn't I say we'd have real, proper adventures? And wasn't I right? "

Well—he certainly was!

THE END

SMUGGLER BEN

CONTENTS

CHAPTER 1

THE COTTAGE BY THE SEA

THREE CHILDREN got out of a bus and looked round them in excitement. Their mother smiled to see their glowing faces.

"Well, here we are!" she said. "How do you like it?"

"Is this the cottage we're going to live in for four weeks?" said Alec, going up to the little white gate. "Mother! It's perfect!"

The two girls, Hilary and Frances, looked at the small square cottage, and agreed with their brother. Red roses climbed all over the cottage even to the chimneys. The thatched roof came down low over

the ground-floor windows, and in the thatch itself
other little windows jutted out.

" I wonder which is our bedroom," said Hilary,
looking up at the roof. " I hope that one is—
because it will look out over the sea."

" Well, let's go in and see," said Mother.
" Help with the suitcases, Alec. I hope the heavy
luggage has already arrived."

They opened the white gate of Sea Cottage and
went up the little stone path. It was set with orange
marigolds at each side, and hundreds of the bright
red-gold flowers looked up at the children as they
passed.

The cottage was very small inside. The front
door opened straight on to the little sitting-room.
Beyond was a tiny dark kitchen. To the left was
another room, whose walls were covered with
bookshelves lined with books. The children stared
at them in surprise.

" The man who owns this house is someone who
is interested in olden times," said Mother, " so
most of these books are about long-ago days, I
expect. They belong to Professor Rondel. He
said that you might dip into any of the books if
you liked, on condition that you put them back
very carefully in the right place."

" Well, I don't think _I_ shall want to do any dipping into these books! " said Hilary.

" No—dipping in the sea will suit _you_ better! "
laughed Frances. " Mother, let's see our bedrooms
now."

They went upstairs. There were three bedrooms,

one very tiny indeed. Two were at the front and one was at the back. A small one and a large one were at the front, and a much bigger one behind.

" I shall have this big one," said Mother. " Then if Daddy comes down there will be plenty of room for him, too. Alec, you can have the tiny room overlooking the sea. And you two girls can have the one next to it."

" That overlooks the sea, too! " said Hilary joyfully. " But, Mother—wouldn't *you* like a room that looks out over the sea? Yours won't."

" I shall see the sea out of this little side window," said Mother, going to it. " And anyway, I shall get a wonderful view of the moors at the back. You know how I love them, especially now when the heather is out."

The children gazed out at the moors ablaze with purple heather. It was really a lovely spot.

" Blue sea in front and purple heather behind," said Alec. " What can anyone want better than that? "

" Well—tea for one thing," said Frances. " I'm most terribly hungry. Mother, could we have something to eat before we do anything? "

" If you like," said Mother. " We can do the unpacking afterwards. Alec, there is a tiny village down the road there, with about two shops and a few fishermen's cottages. Go with the girls and see if you can buy something for tea."

They clattered down the narrow wooden stair-way and ran out of the front door and down the path between the marigolds. They went down the sandy road, where blue chicory blossomed by the wayside and red poppies danced.

"Isn't it heavenly!" cried Hilary. "We're at the seaside—and the holidays are just beginning. We've never been to such a lovely little place before. It's much, much nicer than the big places we've been to. I don't want bands and piers and steamers and things. I only want the yellow sands, and big rocky cliffs, and water as blue as this."

"I vote we go down to the beach after tea, when we've helped Mother to unpack," said Alec. "The tide will be going out then. It comes right up to the cliffs now. Look at it splashing high up the rocks!"

The children peered over the edge of the cliff and saw the white spray flying high. It was lovely to watch. The gulls soared above their heads, making laughing cries as they went.

"I would love to be a gull for a little while," said Frances longingly. "Just think how glorious it would be to glide along on the wind like that for ages and ages. Sometimes I dream I'm doing that."

"So do I," said Hilary. "It's a lovely feeling. Well, come on. It's no good standing here when we're getting things for tea. I'm awfully hungry."

"You always are," said Alec. "I never knew such a girl. All right—come on, Frances. We can do all the exploring we want to after tea."

They ran off. Sand got into their shoes, but they liked it. It was all part of the seaside, and there wasn't anything at the sea that they didn't like. They felt very happy.

They came to the village—though really it could hardly be called a village. There were two shops. One was a tiny baker's, which was also the little post office. The other was a general store that sold everything from pokers to strings of sausages. It was a most fascinating shop.

" It even sells foreign stamps," said Alec, looking at some packets in the window. " And look—that's a fine boat. I might buy that if I've got enough money."

Hilary went to the baker's. She bought a large crusty loaf, a big cake and some currant buns. She asked for their butter and jam at the other store. The little old lady who served her smiled at the children.

" So you've come to Sea Cottage, have you? " she said. " Well, I hope you have a good holiday. And mind you come along to see me every day, for I sell sweets, chocolates and ice-creams, as well as all the other things you see."

" Oooh! " said Hilary. " Well, we'll certainly come and see you then! "

They had a look at the other little cottages in the village. Fishing-nets were drying outside most of them, and one or two of them were being mended. A boy of about Alec's age was mending one. He stared at the children as they passed. They didn't know whether to smile or not.

" He looks a bit fierce, doesn't he? " said Hilary. They looked back at the boy. He did look rather fierce. He was very, very dark, and his face and hands were burnt almost black. He wore an old blue jersey and long trousers, rather ragged, which he had tied up at the ankles. He was bare-footed, but beside him were big sea-boots.

"I don't think I like him much," said Frances. "He looks rather rough."

"Well, he won't bother *us* much," said Alec. "He's only a fisher-boy. Anyway, if he starts to be rough, *I* shall be rough, too—and he won't like that!"

"You wouldn't be nearly as strong as that fisher-boy," said Hilary.

"Yes, I would!" said Alec at once.

"No, you wouldn't," said Hilary. "I bet he's got muscles like iron!"

"Shut up, you two," said Frances. "Don't quarrel on our very first day here."

"All right," said Alec. "It's too lovely a day to quarrel. Come on—let's get back home. I want my tea."

They sat in the garden to have their tea. Mother had brought out a table and stools, and the four of them sat there happily, eating big crusty slices of bread and butter and jam, watching the white tops of the blue waves as they swept up the shore.

"The beach looks a bit dangerous for bathing," said Mother. "I'm glad you are all good swimmers. Alec, you must see that you find out what times are best for bathing. Don't let the girls go in if it's dangerous."

"We can just wear bathing-costumes, Mother, can't we?" said Alec. "And go barefoot?"

"Well, you won't want to go barefoot on those

rocky cliffs, surely!" said Mother. "You can do as you like. But just be sensible, that's all."

"We'll help you to unpack now," said Hilary, getting up.

"Gracious, Hilary—you don't mean to say you've had enough tea yet?" said Alec, pretending to be surprised. "You've only had seven pieces of bread and jam, three pieces of cake and two currant buns!"

Hilary pulled Alec's hair hard and he yelled. Then they all went indoors. Mother said she would clear away the tea when they had gone down to the beach.

In half an hour all the unpacking was done and the children were free to go down to the beach. The tide was now out quite a long way and there was plenty of golden sand to run on.

"Come on!" said Alec impatiently. "Let's go. We won't change into bathing things now, it will waste time. We'll go as we are!"

So off they sped, down the marigold path, through the white gate, and into the sandy lane. A small path led across the grassy cliff-top to where steep steps had been cut in the cliff itself in order that people might get up and down.

"Down we go!" said Alec. "My word—doesn't the sea look grand! I've never seen it so blue in my life!"

CHAPTER 2

A HORRID BOY—AND A DISAPPOINTMENT

THEY REACHED the beach. It was wet from the tide and gleamed brightly as they walked on it. Their feet made little prints on it that faded almost as soon as they were made. Gleaming shells lay here and there, as pink as sunset.

There were big rocks sticking up everywhere, and around them were deep and shallow pools. The children loved paddling in them because they were so warm. They ran down to the edge of the sea and let the white edges of the waves curl over their toes. It was all lovely.

"The fishing-boats are out," said Alec, shading his eyes as he saw the boats setting out on the tide, their white sails gleaming in the sun. " And listen —is that a motor boat? "

It was. One came shooting by at a great pace, and then another. They came from the big seaside town not far off where many trippers went. The children watched them fly past, the white spray flying into the air.

They wandered along by the sea, exploring all the rock pools, picking up shells and splashing in the edge of the water. They saw nobody at all until they rounded a rocky corner of the beach and came to a small cove, well hidden between two jutting-out arms of the cliff.

They heard the sound of whistling, and stopped. Sitting beside a small boat, doing something to it, was the fisher-boy they had seen before tea.

He now had on his sea-boots, a red fisherman's cap with a tassel hanging down, and a bright red scarf tied round his trousers.

" That's the same boy we saw before," said Alec.

The boy heard the sound of voices on the breeze and looked up. He scowled, and his dark face looked savage. He stood up and looked threateningly towards the three children.

" Well, he looks fiercer than ever," said Hilary at last. " What's the matter with him, I wonder? He doesn't look at all pleased to see us."

" Let's go on and take no notice of him," said Alec. " He's no right to glare at us like that. We're doing no harm! "

So the three children walked into the hidden cove, not looking at the fisher-boy at all. But as soon as they had taken three or four steps, the boy shouted at them loudly.

" Hey, you there! Keep out of this cove! "

The children stopped. " Why should we? " said Alec.

" Because it belongs to me," said the boy. " You keep out of this. It's been my cove for years, and no one's come here. I won't have you trippers coming into it and spoiling it."

" We're *not* trippers! " cried Hilary indignantly. " We're staying at Sea Cottage for a whole month."

" Well, you're trippers for a month then instead of for a day! " said the boy sulkily. " Clear off! I tell you. This is my own place here. I don't want anyone else in it. If you come here I'll set on you and beat you off."

The boy really looked so fierce that the children felt quite frightened. Then out of his belt he took a gleaming knife. That settled things for the two girls. They weren't going to have any quarrel with a savage boy who held such a sharp knife.

But Alec was furious. " How dare you threaten us with a knife! " he shouted. " You're a coward. I haven't a knife or I'd fight you."

" Alec! Come away! " begged Frances, clutching hold of her brother. " Do come away. I think that boy's mad. He looks it anyway."

The boy stood watching them, feeling the sharp edge of his knife with his thumb. His sullen face looked as black as thunder.

Frances and Hilary dragged Alec off round the

rocky corner. He struggled with them to get free, and they tore his flannel shirt.

" Now look what you've done! " he cried angrily. " Let me go! "

" Alec, it's seven o'clock already and Mother said we were to be back by then," said Hilary, looking at her watch. " Let's go back. We can settle with that horrid boy another day."

Alec shook himself free and set off home with the girls rather sulkily. He felt that the evening had been spoilt. It had all been so lovely—and now that nasty boy had spoilt everything.

The girls told their mother about the boy, and she was astonished. " Well, he certainly does sound rather mad," she said. " For goodness' sake don't start quarrelling with him. Leave him alone."

" But, Mother, if he won't let us go into the little coves, it's not fair," said Hilary.

Mother laughed. " Don't worry about that! " she said. " There will be plenty of times when he's busy elsewhere, and the places you want to go to will be empty. Sometimes the people who live in a place do resent others coming to stay in it for a while."

" Mother, could we have a boat, do you think? " asked Alec. " It would be such fun."

" I'll go and see about one for you to-morrow," said Mother. " Now it's time you all went to bed. Hilary is yawning so widely that I can almost count her teeth! "

They were all tired. They fell into bed and went to sleep at once, although Hilary badly wanted to lie awake for a time and listen to the lovely noise the sea made outside her window. But she simply couldn't keep her eyes open, and in about half a minute she was as sound asleep as the other two.

It was lovely to wake up in the morning and remember everything. Frances woke first and sat up. She saw the blue sea shining in the distance and she gave Hilary a sharp dig.

"Hilary! Wake up! We're at the seaside!"

Hilary woke with a jump. She sat up, too, and gazed out to the sea, over which white gulls were soaring. She felt so happy that she could hardly speak. Then Alec appeared at the door in his bathing-trunks. He had nothing else on at all, and his face was excited.

"I'm going for a dip," he said in a low voice. "Are you coming? Don't wake Mother. It's early."

The girls almost fell out of bed in their excitement. They pulled on bathing-dresses, and then crept out of the cottage with Alec.

It was about half-past six. The world looked clean and new. "Just as if it has been freshly washed," said Hilary, sniffing the sharp, salt breeze. "Look at those pink clouds over there! And did you ever see such a clear blue as the sea is this morning. Ooooh—it's cold!"

It *was* cold. The children ran into the water a little way and then stopped and shivered. Alec plunged right under and came up, shaking the drops from his hair. "Come on!" he yelled. "It's gorgeous once you're in!"

The girls were soon right under, and the three of them spent twenty minutes swimming out and back, diving under the water and catching each other's legs, then floating happily on their backs, looking up into the clear morning sky.

" Time to come out," said Alec at last. " Come on. Race you up the cliff! "

But they had to go slowly up the cliff, for the steps really were very steep. They burst into the cottage to find Mother up and bustling round to get breakfast ready.

At half-past seven they were all having breakfast. Afterwards Mother said she would tidy round the house and then do the shopping. The girls and Alec must make their own beds, just as they did at home.

" When we are down in the village I'll make inquiries about a boat for you," promised Mother, when at last the beds were made, the kitchen and sitting-room tidied and set in order. " Now, are we ready? Bring that big basket, Alec. I shall want that."

" Mother, we must buy spades," said Alec. " That sand would be gorgeous to dig in."

" Gracious! Aren't you too big to dig? " said Mother. The children laughed.

" Mother, you're not too big either! Don't you remember how you helped us to dig that simply enormous castle last year, with the big moat round it? It had steps all the way up it and was simply lovely."

They set off joyously, Alec swinging the basket.

They did a lot of shopping at the little general store, and the little old lady beamed at them.

" Do you know where I can arrange about hiring a boat for my children? " Mother asked her.

" Well," said the old lady, whose name was Mrs. Polsett, " I really don't know. We use all our boats hereabouts, you know. You could ask Samuel. He lives in the cottage over yonder. He's got a small boat as well as a fishing-boat. Maybe he'd let the children have it."

So Mother went across to where Samuel was sitting mending a great fishing-net. He was an old man with bright blue eyes and a wrinkled face like a shrivelled brown apple. He touched his forehead when Mother spoke to him.

" Have you a boat I could hire for my children? " Mother asked.

Samuel shook his head. " No, Mum," he said. "I have got one, it's true—but I'm not hiring it out any more. Some boys had it last year, and they lost the oars and made a great hole in the bottom. I lost more money on that there boat than I made."

" Well, I'm sure my three children would be very careful indeed," said Mother, seeing the disappointed faces around her. " Won't you lend it to them for a week and see how they get on? I will pay you well."

" No, thank you kindly, Mum," said Samuel firmly.

" Is there anyone else who has a boat to spare? " said Alec, feeling rather desperate, for he had really set his heart on a boat.

"No one that I know of," said Samuel. "Some of us lost our small boats in a big storm this year, when the sea came right over the cliffs, the waves were so big. Maybe I'll take the children out in my fishing-boat if they're well behaved."

"Thank you," said Hilary. But they all looked very disappointed, because going out in somebody else's boat wasn't a bit the same as having their own.

"We'll just go back to old Mrs. Polsett's shop and see if she knows of anyone else with a boat," said Mother. So back they went.

But the old lady shook her head.

"The only other person who has a boat—and it's not much of a boat, all patched and mended," she said, "is Smuggler Ben."

"Smuggler Ben!" said Alec. "Is there a smuggler here? Where does he live?"

"Oh, he's not a real smuggler!" said Mrs. Polsett, with a laugh. "He's my grandson. But he's just mad on tales of the old-time smugglers, and he likes to pretend he's one. There were smugglers' caves here, you know, somewhere about the beach. I dare say Ben knows them. Nobody else does now."

The children felt terribly excited. Smugglers— and caves! And who was Smuggler Ben? They felt that they would very much like to know him. And he had a boat, too. He would be a fine person to know!

"Is Smuggler Ben grown-up?" asked Alec.

"Bless you, no!" said Mrs. Polsett. "He's

much about the same age as you. Look—there he goes—down the street there!"

The children turned to look. And as soon as they saw the boy, their hearts sank.

"It's the nasty boy with the knife!" said Hilary sadly. "*He* won't lend us his boat."

"Don't you worry about his knife," said old Mrs. Polsett. "It's all pretence with him. He's just play-acting most of the time. He always wishes he could have been a smuggler, and he's for ever pretending he is one. There's no harm in him. He's a good boy for work—and when he wants to play, well, let him play as he likes, I say! He doesn't get into mischief like most boys do. He goes off exploring the cliffs, and rows in his boat half the time. But he does keep himself to himself. Shall I ask him if he'll lend you his boat sometimes?"

"No, thank you," said Alec politely. He was sure the boy would refuse rudely, and Alec wasn't going to give him the chance to do that.

They walked back to Sea Cottage. They felt sad about the boat—but their spirits rose as they saw their bathing-costumes lying on the grass, bone-dry.

"What about another bathe before lunch?" cried Alec. "Come on, Mother. You must come, too!"

So down to the sea they all went again, and by the squeals, shrieks and shouts, four people had a really wonderful time!

CHAPTER 3

HILARY HAS AN ADVENTURE

ONE EVENING, after tea, Frances and Alec wanted to go for a long walk. " Coming, Hilary? " they said. Hilary shook her head.

" No," she said. " I'm a bit tired with all my swimming to-day. I'll take a book and go and sit on the cliff-top till you come back."

So Alec went off with Frances, and Hilary took her book and went to find a nice place to sit. She could see miles and miles of restless blue sea from the cliff. It was really marvellous. She walked on the cliff-edge towards the east, found a big gorse bush and sat down beside it for shelter. She opened her book.

When she looked up, something nearby caught her eye. It looked like a little-worn path going straight to the cliff-edge. "A rabbit path, I suppose," said Hilary to herself. "But fancy the rabbits going right over the steep cliff-edge like that! I suppose there must be a hole there that they pop into."

She got up to look—and to her great surprise saw what looked like a narrow, rocky path going down the cliff-side, very steep indeed! In a sandy ledge a little way down was the print of a bare foot.

"Well, *someone* has plainly gone down this steep path!" thought Hilary. "I wonder who it was. I wonder where it leads to. I've a good mind to find out! "

She began to go down the path. It really was very steep and rather dangerous. At one extremely dangerous part someone had driven in iron bars and stretched a piece of strong rope from bar to bar. Hilary was glad to get hold of it, for her feet were sliding down by themselves and she was afraid she was going to fall.

When she was about three-quarters of the way down she heard the sound of someone whistling very quietly. She stopped and tried to peer down to see who was on the beach.

"Why, this path leads down to that little cove we saw the other day!" she thought excitedly. "The one where the rude boy was. Oh, I hope he isn't there now! "

He was! He was sitting on his upturned boat, whittling at something with his sharp knife. Hilary turned rather pale when she saw the knife. It was all very well for old Mrs. Polsett to say that her grandson was only play-acting—but Hilary was sure that Ben really felt himself to be somebody fierce—and he might act like that, too.

As she stood and watched him, unseen, she saw the sharp knife slip. The boy gave a cry of pain and clutched his left hand. He had cut it very badly indeed. Blood began to drip on to the sand.

The boy felt in his pocket for something to bind up his hand. But he could find nothing. He pressed the cut together, but it went on bleeding. Hilary was tender-hearted and she couldn't bear to see the boy's face all screwed up in pain, and do nothing about it.

She forgot to be afraid of him. She went down the last piece of cliff and jumped down on the sand. The boy heard her and turned, his face one big scowl. Hilary ran up to him.

She had a big clean handkerchief in her pocket, and she took this out. " I'll tie up your hand for you," she said. " I say—what an *awful* cut! I should howl like anything if I did that to myself."

The boy scowled at her again. " What are you doing here? " he said. " Where are the others? "

" I'm alone," said Hilary. " I found that funny steep path and came down it to see where it led to. And I saw you cut your hand. Give it to me. Come on, Ben—hold it out and let me tie it up. You might bleed to death if you go on like this."

The boy held out his cut hand. " How do you

know my name is Ben? " he said, in a surly voice.

" Never mind how I know! " said Hilary. " You're Smuggler Ben! What a marvellous name! Don't you wish you really *were* a smuggler? I do! I'm just reading a book about smuggling and it's terribly exciting."

" What book? " asked the boy.

Hilary bound up his hand well, and then showed him the book. " It's all about hidden caves and smugglers coming in at night and things like that," she said. " I'll lend it to you if you like."

The boy stared at her. He couldn't help liking this little girl with her straight eyes and clear, kind little voice. His hand felt much more comfortable now, too. He was grateful to her. He took the book and looked through the pages.

" I'd like to read it after you," he said, more graciously. " I can't get enough books. Do you really like smuggling and that kind of thing? "

" Of course," said Hilary. " I like anything adventurous like that. Is it true that there are smuggler's caves along this coast somewhere? "

The boy stopped before he answered. " If I tell you, will you keep it a secret? " he said at last.

" Well—I could tell the others, couldn't I? " said Hilary. " We all share everything, you know, Alec and Frances and I."

" No, I don't want you to tell anyone," said the boy. " It's my own secret. I wouldn't mind sharing it with you, because you've helped me, and you like smuggling, too. But I don't want the others to know."

"Then don't tell me," said Hilary, disappointed. "You see, it would be mean of me to keep an exciting thing like that from the others. I just couldn't do it. You'd know how I feel if you had brothers and sisters. You just have to share exciting things."

"I haven't got any brothers or sisters," said the boy. "I wish I had. I always play alone. There aren't any boys of my age in our village—only girls, and I don't like girls. They're silly."

"Oh well, if you think that, I'll go," said Hilary offended. She turned to go, but the boy caught her arm.

"No, don't go. I didn't mean that *you* were silly. I don't think you are. I think you're sensible. Let me tell you one of my secrets."

"Not unless I can share it with the others," said Hilary. "I'm simply longing to know—but I don't want to leave the others out of it."

"Are they as sensible as you are?" asked Ben.

"Of course," said Hilary. "As a matter of fact, Frances, my sister, is nicer than I am. I'm always losing my temper and she doesn't. You can trust us, Ben, really you can."

"Well," said Ben slowly, "I'll let you all into my secret then. I'll show you something that will make you stare! Come here to-morrow, down that little path. I'll be here, and just see if I don't astonish you."

Hilary's eyes shone. She felt excited. She caught hold of Ben's arm and looked at him eagerly.

"You're a sport!" she said. "I like you,

Smuggler Ben. Let's all be smugglers, shall we?"

Ben smiled for the first time. His brown face changed completely, and his dark eyes twinkled. "All right," he said. "We'll all be. That would be more fun than playing alone, if I can trust you all not to say a word to any grown-up. They might interfere. And now I'll tell you one little secret—and you can tell the others if you like. I know where the old smugglers' caves are!"

"Ben!" cried Hilary, her eyes shining with excitement. "Do you really? I wondered if you did. Oh, I say, isn't that simply marvellous! Will you show us them to-morrow? Oh, do say you will."

"You wait and see," said Ben. He turned his boat the right way up and dragged it down the beach.

"Where are you going?" called Hilary.

"Back home in my boat," said Ben. "I've got to go out fishing with my uncle to-night. Would you like to come back in my boat with me? It'll save you climbing up that steep path."

"Oh, I'd love to!" said Hilary joyfully. "You know, Ben, we tried and tried to hire a boat of our own, but we couldn't. We were so terribly disappointed. Can I get in? You push her out."

Ben pushed the boat out on to the waves and then got in himself. But when he took the oars he found that his cut hand was far too painful to handle the left oar. He bit his lip and went a little pale under his tan.

"What's the matter?" said Hilary. "Oh, it's

your hand. Well, let me take the oars. I can row. Yes, I can, Ben! You'll only make your cut bleed again."

Ben gave up his seat and the girl took the oars. She rowed very well indeed, and the oars cut cleanly into the water. The boat flew along over the waves.

" You don't row badly for a girl," said Ben.

" Well, we live near a river at home," said Hilary, " and we are often out in our uncle's boat. We can all row. So you can guess how disappointed we were when we found that we couldn't get a boat here for ouselves."

Ben was silent for a little while. Then he spoke again. " Well—I don't mind lending you my boat sometimes, if you like. When I'm out fishing, you can have it—but don't you dare to spoil it in any way. I know it's only an old boat, but I love it."

Hilary stopped rowing and looked at Ben in delight. " I say, you really are a brick! " she said. " Do you mean it? "

" I always mean what I say," said Ben gruffly. " You lend me your books—and I'll lend you my boat."

Hilary rowed all round the cliffs until she came to the beach she knew. She rowed inshore and the two got out. She and Ben pulled the boat right up the beach and turned it upside down.

" I must go now," said Ben. " My uncle's waiting for me. See you to-morrow."

He went off, and Hilary turned to go home. At the top of the beach she saw Frances and Alec staring at her in amazement.

" Hilary! Were you with that awful boy in his
boat? " cried Frances. " However did you dare? "

" He isn't awful after all," said Hilary. " He's
quite nice. He's got wonderful secrets—simply
wonderful. And he says we can use his boat when
he doesn't want it! "

The other two stared open-mouthed. They
simply couldn't believe all this. Why, that boy
had threatened them with a knife—he couldn't
possibly be nice enough to lend them his boat.

" I'll tell you all about it," said Hilary, as they
set off up the cliff-path. " You see, I found a
little secret way down to that cove we saw—and
Ben was there."

She told them the whole story and they listened
in silence.

" Things always happen to you, Hilary," said
Frances, rather enviously. " Well, I must say this
is all very exciting. I can hardly wait till to-
morrow. Do you really think Smuggler Ben will
show us those caves? I wonder where they are?
I hope they aren't miles away! "

" Well, we'll see," said Hilary happily. They
went home hungry to their supper—and in bed
that night each of them dreamt of caves and
smugglers and all kinds of exciting things. This
holiday promised to be more thrilling than they
had imagined!

CHAPTER 4

AN EXCITING EVENING

THE CHILDREN told their mother about Ben. She was amused.

"So the fierce little boy has turned out to be quite ordinary after all!" she said. "Well, I must say I'm glad. I didn't very much like to think of a little savage rushing about the shore armed with a sharp knife. I think it's very nice of him to lend you his boat. You had better bring him in to a meal, and then I can see him for myself."

"Oh, thanks, Mother," said Hilary. "I say— do you think we could get ourselves some fishermen's hats, like Ben wears—and have you got a bright-coloured scarf or sash that you could lend us, Mother? Or three, if you've got them. We're going to play smugglers, and it would be fun to dress up a bit. Ben does. He looks awfully grand in his tasselled hat and sash and big boots."

" Hilary, you don't seriously think I am going to hand you out all my precious scarves, do you? " said Mother. " I'll give you some money to go and buy three cheap hats and scarves with, if you like—and you can all wear your wellingtons if you want big boots. But I draw the line at getting you sharp knives like Ben. Look how even he cut himself to-day! "

The children were delighted to think they could buy something they could dress up in. The next morning they set off to Mrs. Polsett's and asked to see fishermen's hats. She had a few and brought them out. " I knitted them myself," she said. " Here's a red one with a yellow tassel. That would suit you fine, Miss Hilary."

So it did. Hilary pulled it on and swung the tasselled end over her left ear just as she had seen Ben do.

Frances chose a blue one with a red tassel and Alec chose a green one with a brown tassel. Then they bought some very cheap scarves to tie round their waists.

They went back home, pulled on their wellingtons, and put on their hats and sashes.

They looked grand.

Hilary showed them where the little narrow path ran down the steep cliff.

" Goodness," said Alec, peering over the edge.

"What a terrifying way down! I feel half-afraid of falling. I'm sure I can never get down those steep bits."

"There's a rope tied there," said Hilary, going down first. "Come on. Ben will be waiting. I saw his boat out on the water as we came along the cliff."

They all went down the path, slowly for fear of falling. When they jumped down the last rocky step into the little cove, they saw Ben there waiting for them, sitting on his little boat. He was dressed just as they were, except that his boots were real seaboots, and he wore trousers tucked well down into them. He didn't move as they came up, nor did he smile.

"Hallo, Ben!" said Hilary. "I've brought my brother and sister as you said I could. This is Alec, and this is Frances. I've told them what you said. We're all terribly excited."

"Did you tell them it's all a deep secret?" said Ben, looking at Hilary. "They won't give it away?"

"Of course we won't," said Alec indignantly. "That would spoil all the fun. I say—can we call you Smuggler Ben? It sounds fine."

Ben looked pleased. "Yes, you can," he said. "And remember, I'm the captain. You've got to obey my orders."

"Oh," said Alec, not liking this idea quite so much. "Well—all right. Lead on. Show us your secret."

"You know, don't you, that there really were

smugglers here in the old days? " said Ben. " They came up the coast quietly on dark nights, bringing in all kinds of goods. Folk here knew they came, but they were afraid of them. They used to take the goods to the old caves here, and hide them there till they could get rid of them overland."

" And do you really know where the caves are? " said Alec eagerly. " My word, Smuggler Ben— you're a wonder! "

Smuggler Ben smiled and his brown face changed at once. " Come on," he said. " I'll show you something that will surprise you! "

He led the way up the beach to the cliffs at the back. " Now," he said, " the entrance to the old caves is somewhere in this little cove. Before I show you, see if you can find it! "

" In this cove! " cried Hilary. " Oh, I guess we shall soon find it then! "

The three children began to hunt carefully along the rocky cliff. They ran into narrow caves and out again. They came to a big cave, went into that and came out again. It seemed nothing but a large cave, narrowing at the back. There were no more caves after that one, and the children turned in disappointment to Ben.

" You don't mean that these little caves and that one big one are the old smuggling caves do you? " said Hilary. " Because they are just like heaps of other caves we have seen at the seaside."

" No, I don't mean that," said Ben. " Now you come with me and I'll show you something exciting."

He led them into the big cave. He took them to the right of it and then jumped up to a rocky ledge which was just about shoulder high. In half a moment he had completely disappeared! Hilary felt about on the ledge and called to him in bewilderment.

" Ben! Smuggler Ben! Where have you gone? "

There was no answer. The three children stared up at the ledge. Alec jumped up to it. He felt all along it, up and down and sideways. He simply couldn't imagine where Ben had gone to!

There was a low laugh behind them. The children turned in surprise—and there was Ben, standing at the entrance to the big cave, laughing all over his brown face at their surprise.

" Ben! What happened? Where did you disappear to? And how did you get back to the entrance without us seeing you? " cried Hilary. " It's like magic. Do tell us. Quick! "

" Well, I'll show you," said Ben. " I found it out quite by accident. One day I came into this cave and fell asleep. When I woke up, the tide was high and was already coming into the cave. I was trapped. I couldn't possibly get out, because I knew I'd be dashed to pieces against the rocks outside, the sea was so stormy."

" So you climbed up on to this ledge! " cried Hilary.

" Yes, I did," said Ben. " It was the only thing to do. I just hoped and hoped the sea wouldn't fill the cave up completely, or I knew I'd be drowned. Well, I crouched there for ages, the sea getting higher and higher up till it reached that ledge."

" Gracious! " said Frances, shivering. " You must have been afraid."

" I was, rather," said Ben. " Well, I rolled right to the back of the ledge, and put up my hand to catch hold of any bit of jutting-out rock that I could—and instead of knocking against rock, my hand went into space! "

" What do you mean? " said Alec, in astonishment.

" Come and see," said Ben, and he took a torch out of his pocket. All the children climbed on to the ledge, and squeezed together there, watching the beam of Ben's torch. He directed it upwards —and then, to their amazement, they saw a perfectly round hole going upwards right at the far corner of the rocky ledge. It didn't look very big.

" See that? " said Ben. " Well, when I felt my hand going up that hole I slid over to this corner and put my arm right up the hole. And this is is what I found."

He shone his torch up the rounded hole in the rock. The three children peered up, one after another.

Driven into the rock were great thick nails, one above the other. " See those? " said Ben. " Well, I reckon they were put there by some old-time smuggler."

" Did you get up the hole? " asked Alec.

" You bet I did! " said Ben. " And pretty quick, too, for the sea was washing inches above

"Real *smugglers* have been here!" said Hilary, in a whisper the ledge by that time and I was soaked through. I squeezed myself up, got my feet on those nails —they're sort of steps up, you see—and climbed up the hole by feeling for the nails with my feet."

" Where does the hole lead to? " asked Frances, in excitement.

" You'd better come and see," said Ben, with a sudden grin. The children asked nothing better than that, and at once Alec put his head up the hole. It was not such a tight fit as he expected. He was easily able to climb up. There were about twenty nails for footholds and then they stopped. There was another ledge to climb out on. The boy dragged himself there, and looked down.

" Can't see a thing! " he called. " Come on up, Smuggler Ben, and bring your torch."

" I'll give Hilary my torch," said Ben. " She can shine it for you up there when she's up, and shine it down for us to climb up by, too. Go on, Hilary."

So Hilary went up next with the torch—and when she shone it around her at the top, she and Alec gave a shout of astonishment.

They were on a ledge near the ceiling of a most enormous cave. It looked almost as big as a church to the children. The floor was of rock, not of sand. Queer lights shone in the walls. They came from the twinkling bits of metal in the rocks.

" Frances! Hurry," cried Hilary. " It's marvellous here."

Soon all four children were standing on the ledge, looking down into the great cave. In it, on the floor, were many boxes of all kinds—small, big, square, oblong. Bits of rope were scattered about, too, and an old broken lantern lay in a corner.

"*Real* smugglers have been here!" said Hilary, in a whisper.

"What are you whispering for?" said Alec, with a laugh. "Afraid they will hear you?"

"No—but it all seems so mysterious," said Hilary. "Let's get down to the floor of the cave. How do we get there?"

"Jump," said Ben.

So they jumped. They ran to the boxes and opened the lids.

"No good," said Ben. "I've done that long ago. They're quite empty. I often come to play smugglers here when I'm by myself. Isn't it a fine place?"

"Simply marvellous!" said Alec. "Let's all come here and play to-morrow. We can bring candles and something to eat and drink. It would be gorgeous."

"Oooh, yes," said Hilary. So they planned everything in excitement, and then climbed back to the ledge, and down through the hole into the first cave. Out they went into the sunshine. Ben smiled as much as the rest.

"It's fun to share my secret with you," he told the others half shyly. "It will be grand to play smugglers all together, instead of just by myself. I'll bring some sandwiches to-morrow, and some plums. You bring anything you can, too. It shall be our own secret smuggler's cave—and we're the smugglers!"

CHAPTER 5

YET ANOTHER SECRET

THE NEXT day the four children met together in the big cave. They felt very thrilled as they climbed up the hole and then jumped down into the smuggler's cave. They had brought candles and food with them, and Alec had bottles of home-made lemonade on his back in a leather bag.

They played smugglers to their hearts' content. Ben ordered them about, and called them " My men," and everyone enjoyed the game thoroughly. At last Alec sat down on a big box and said he was tired of playing.

" I'd like something to eat," he said. " Let's use this big box for a table."

They set the things out on the table. And then Hilary looked in a puzzled way at the box.

" What's up? " asked Alec, seeing her look.

" Well, I'm just wondering something," said Hilary. " How in the world did the smugglers get this big box up the small round hole to this cave? After all, that hole only just takes us comfortably —surely this box would never have got through it."

Frances and Alec stared at the box. They felt puzzled, too. It was quite certain that no one could have carried such a big box through the hole. They looked at Ben.

" Have you ever thought of that! " Alec asked him.

" Plenty of times," said Ben. " And, what's more, I know the answer! "

" Tell us! " begged Hilary. " Is there another way into this cave? "

Smuggler Ben nodded. " Yes," he said. " I'll show it to you if you like. I just wanted to see if any of my three men were clever enough to think of such a thing. Come on—I'll show you the other way in. Didn't you wonder yesterday how it was that I came back into the other cave after I'd disappeared up the hole? "

He stood up and the others rose, too, all excited. Ben went to the back of the cave. It seemed to the children as if the wall there was quite continuous —but it wasn't. There was a fold in it—and in the fold was a passage! It was wide, but low, and the children had to crouch down almost double to get into it. But almost immediately it rose high and they could stand. Smuggler Ben switched on his torch, and the children saw that the passage was quite short and led into yet another cave. This was small and ran right down to the rocky side of the cliff very steeply, more like a wide passage than a cave.

The children went down the long cave and came to a rocky inlet of water. " When the tide comes in, it sweeps right through this cave," said Ben, " and I reckon that this is where the smugglers brought in their goods—by boat. The boat would be guided into this watery passage at high tide, and beached at the far end, where the tide didn't reach. Then the things could easily be taken into the big cave. The smugglers left a way of escape for themselves down the hole we climbed through from the first cave—you know, where the nails are driven into the rock."

" This gets more and more exciting! " said Alec. " Anything more, Ben? Don't keep it from us. Tell us everything! "

" Well, there is one thing more," said Ben, " but it just beats me. Maybe the four of us together could do something about it though. Come along and I'll show you."

He led them back to the little passage between the big cave and the one they were in. He climbed up the wall a little way, and then disappeared. The others followed him.

There was another passage leading off into the darkness there, back into the cliff. Ben shone his torch down it as the others crowded on his heels.

" Let's go up it! " cried Alec excitedly.

" We can't," said Ben, and he shone his torch before him. " The passage walls have fallen in just along there—look! "

So they had. The passage ended in a heap of stones, soil and sand. It was completely blocked up.

" Can't we clear it? " cried Alec.

" Well, we might, as there are so many of us," said Ben. " I didn't feel like tackling it all by myself, I must say. For one thing I didn't know how far back the passage was blocked. It might have fallen in for a long way."

" I wonder where it leads to," said Alec. " It seems to go straight back. I say—isn't this thrilling! "

" We'll come and dig it out to-morrow," said Hilary, her eyes dancing. " We'll bring our spades—and a sack or something to put the stones and soil in. Then we can drag it away and empty it."

" Be here to-morrow after tea," said Smuggler Ben, laughing. " I'll bring my uncle's big spade. That's a powerful one—it will soon dig away the soil."

So the next day the children crowded into the cave with spades and sacks. They used the ordinary way in, climbing up the hole by the nails and jumping into the cave from the high ledge. Then they made their way into the low passage, and climbed up where the roof rose high, till they came to the blocked-up passage. They went on

by the light of their torches and came to the big
fall of stones and soil.

"Now, men, to work!" said Smuggler Ben,
and the gang set to work with a will. The boys
shovelled away the soil and stones, and the girls
filled the sacks. Then the boys dragged them down
the passage, let them fall to the opening between
the two caves, climbed down, dragged the sacks
into the large cave and emptied them into a corner.
Then back they went again to do some more
digging.

"What's the time?" said Alec at last. "I feel
as if we've been working for hours. We mustn't
forget that high tide is at half-past seven. We've
got to get out before then."

Hilary looked at her watch. "It's all right," she
said. "It's only half-past six. We've plenty of
time."

"Gracious! Hasn't the time gone slowly!"
said Frances in surprise. "Come on—we can do a
lot more!"

They went on working, and after a time Ben
began to feel rather uncomfortable. "Hilary,
what's the time now?" he said. "I'm sure it
must be getting near high tide."

Hilary glanced at her watch again. "It's half-
past six," she said, in surprise.

"But you said that before!" cried Ben. "Has
your watch stopped?"

It had! Hilary held it to her ear and cried out in
dismay. "Yes! It's stopped. Oh, blow! I wonder
what the right time is."

" Quick! We'd better go and see how the tide is," said Ben, and he dropped his spade and rushed to the entrance of the blocked-up passage. He dropped down and went into the big cave, and then climbed up to the ledge, and then down by the nail-studded hole on to the ledge in the first cave.

But even as he climbed down to the ledge, he felt the wash of water over his foot. " Golly! The tide's almost in! " he yelled. " We're caught! We can't get out! "

He climbed back and stood in the big cave with the others. They looked at him, half-frightened.

" Don't be scared," said Smuggler Ben. " It only means we'll have to wait a few hours till the tide goes down. I hope your mother won't worry."

" She's out to-night," said Alec. " She won't know. Does the water come in here, Ben? "

" Of course not," said Ben. " This cave is too high up. Well—let's sit down, have some chocolate and a rest, and then we might as well get on with our job."

Time went on. The boys went to see if the tide was falling, but it was still very high. It was getting dark outside. The boys stood at the end of the long, narrow cave, up which the sea now rushed deeply. And as they stood there, they heard a strange noise coming nearer and nearer.

" Whatever's that? " said Alec, in astonishment.

" It sounds like a motor boat," said Ben.

" It can't be," said Alec.

But it was. A small motor boat suddenly loomed

out of the darkness and worked itself very carefully up the narrow passage and into the long cave, which was now full of deep water! The boys were at first too startled to move. They heard men and women talking in low voices.

" Is this the place? "

" Yes—step out just there. Wait till the wave goes back. That's it—now step out."

Ben clutched hold of Alec's arm and pulled him silently away, back into the entrance between the caves. Up they went in the blocked passage. The girls called out to them: " What's the tide like? "

" Sh! " said Smuggler Ben, so fiercely that the girls were quite frightened. They stared at Ben with big eyes. The boy told them in a whisper what he and Alec had seen.

" Something's going on," he said mysteriously. " I don't know what. But it makes me suspicious when strange motor boats come to our coasts late at night like this and run into a little-known cave. After all, our country is at war—they may be up to no good, these people. They may be enemies! "

All the children felt a shivery feeling down their backs when Ben said this. Hilary felt that it was just a bit *too* exciting. " What do you mean? " she whispered.

" I don't exactly know," said Ben. " All I know for certain is that it's plain somebody else knows of these caves and plans to use them for something. I don't know what. And it's up to us to find out! "

" Oooh! I wish we could! " said Hilary at once.
" What are we going to do now? Wait here? "

" Alec and I will go down to the beginning of
this passage," said Ben. " Maybe the people
don't know about it. We'll see if we can hear what
they say."

So they crept down to the beginning of the
passage and leaned over to listen. Three or four
people had now gone into the big cave, but to
Ben's great disappointment they were talking in a
strange language, and he could not understand a
word.

Then came something he *did* understand! One
of the women spoke in English. " We will bring
them on Thursday night," she said. " When the
tide is full."

Another man answered. Then the people went
back to their motor boat, and the boys soon heard
the whirring of the engine as it made its way carefully out of the long, narrow cave.

" They're using that cave rather like a boat-
house," said Ben. " Golly, I wonder how they
knew about it. And what are they bringing in on
Thursday night? "

" Smuggled goods, do you think? " said Alec,
hot with excitement. " People always smuggle
things in wartime. Mother said so. They're
smugglers, Ben—smugglers of nowadays! And
they're using the old smugglers' caves again. I say
—isn't this awfully exciting? "

" Yes, it is," said Smuggler Ben. " We'd better
come here on Thursday night, Alec. We'll have to

see what happens. We simply must. Can you slip
away about midnight, do you think?"

"Of course!" said Alec. "You bet! And the
girls, too! We'll all be here! And we'll watch to
see exactly what happens. Fancy spying on real
smugglers, Ben. What a thrill!"

CHAPTER 6

A QUEER DISCOVERY

MOTHER WAS in by the time the children got back home, and she was very worried indeed about them.

"Mother, it's all right," said Alec, going over to her. "We just got caught by the tide, that's all, playing in caves. But we were quite safe. We just waited till the tide went down."

"Now listen, Alec," said Mother, "this just won't do. I shall forbid you to play in those caves if you get caught another time, and worry me like this. I imagined you all drowning or something."

"We're awfully sorry, Mother," said Hilary, putting her arms round her. "Really, we wouldn't have worried you for anything. Look—my watch stopped at half-past six, and that put us all wrong about the tide."

"Very well," said Mother. "I'll forgive you this time—but I warn you, if you worry me again like this, you won't be allowed to set foot in a single cave!"

The next day it poured with rain, which was very disappointing. Alec ran down to the village to see what Ben was doing. The two boys talked excitedly about what had happened the night before.

"Mother says will you come and spend the day with us?" said Alec. "Do come. You'll like Mother, she's a dear."

The two boys went back to Sea Cottage. The girls welcomed them, and Mother shook hands with Ben very politely.

"I'm glad you can come for the day," she said. "You'd better go up to the girls' bedroom and play there. I want the sitting-room to do some writing in this morning."

So they all went up to the bedroom above, and sat down to talk. "It's nice of Mother to send us up here," said Hilary. "We can talk in peace. What are our plans for Thursday, Captain?"

"Well, I don't quite know," said Ben slowly. "You see, we've got to be there at midnight, haven't we?—but we simply must be there a good time before that, because of the tide. You see, we can't get into either cave if the tide is up. We'd be dashed to pieces."

The children stared at Smuggler Ben in dismay. None of them had thought of that.

"What time would we have to be there?" asked Alec.

"We'd have to be there about half-past nine, as far as I can reckon," said Ben. "Can you leave by that time? What would your mother say?"

"Mother wouldn't let us, I'm sure of that," said Hilary, in disappointment. "She was so dreadfully worried about us last night. I'm quite sure if we told her what we wanted to do, she would say ' No ' at once."

"She isn't in bed by that time, then?" said Ben.

The children shook their heads. All four were puzzled and disappointed. They couldn't think how to get over the difficulty. There was no way out of the cottage except through the sitting-room door—and Mother would be in the room, writing or reading, at the time they wanted to go out.

"What about getting out of the window?" said Alec, going over to look. But that was quite impossible, too. It was too far to jump, and, any-way, Mother would be sure to hear any noise they made.

"It looks as if I'll have to go alone," said Ben gloomily. "It's funny—I used to like doing every-thing all by myself, you know—but now I don't like it at all. I want to be with my three men!"

"Oh, Ben—it would be awful thinking of you down in those caves finding out what was happening—and us in our bed, wanting and longing to be with you!" cried Hilary.

"Well, I simply don't know what else to do," said Ben. "If you can't come, you can't. And certainly I wouldn't let you come after your mother had gone to bed, because by that time the tide would be up, and you'd simply be washed away as soon as you put foot on the beach. No—I'll go alone—and I'll come and tell you what's happened the next morning."

The children felt terribly disappointed and gloomy. "Let's go downstairs into that little study place that's lined with books," said Hilary at last. "I looked into one of the books the other day, and it seemed to be all about this district in the old days. Maybe we might find some bits about smugglers."

Ben brightened up at once. "That would be fine," he said. "I know Professor Rondel was supposed to have a heap of books about this district. He was a funny man—never talked to anyone. I didn't like him."

The children went downstairs. Mother called out to them: "Where are you going?"

"Into the book-room," said Hilary, opening the sitting-room door. "We may, mayn't we?"

"Yes, but be sure to take care of any book you use, and put it back into its right place," said Mother. They promised this and then went into the little study.

"My word! What hundreds of books!" said Ben, in amazement. The walls were lined with them, almost from floor to ceiling. The boy ran his eyes along the shelves. He picked out a book and looked at it.

" Here's a book about the moors behind here," he said. " And maps, too. Look—I've been along here—and crossed that stream just there."

The children looked. " We ought to go for some walks with you over those lovely moors, Ben," said Alec. " I'd like that."

Hilary took down one or two books and looked through them, too, trying to find something exciting to read. She found nothing and put them back. Frances showed her a book on the top shelf.

" Look," she said, " do you think that would be any good? It's called *Old-Time Smugglers' Haunts*."

" It might be interesting," said Hilary, and stood on a chair to get the book. It was big and old and smelt musty. The girl jumped down with it and opened it on the table. The first picture she saw made her cry out.

" Oh, look—here's an old picture of this village! Here are the cliffs—and there are the old, old houses that the fishermen still live in! "

She was quite right. Underneath the picture was written: " A little-known smugglers' haunt. See page 66."

They turned to page sixty-six, and found printed there an account of the caves in the little cove on the beach. " The best-known smuggler of those days was a dark, fiery man named Smuggler Ben," said the book. The children exclaimed in surprise and looked at Ben.

" How funny! " they cried. " Did you know that, Ben? "

" No," said Ben. " My name is really Benjamin, of course, but everyone calls me Ben. I'm dark, too. I wonder if Smuggler Ben was an ancestor of mine—you know, some sort of relation a hundred or more years ago? "

" Quite likely," said Alec. " I wish we could find a picture of him to see if he's like you."

But they couldn't. They turned over the pages of the book and gave it up. But before they shut it Ben took hold of it. He had an idea.

" I just wonder if by chance there's a mention of that blocked-up passage," he said. " It would be fun to know where it comes out, wouldn't it? "

He looked carefully through the book. He came again to page sixty-six, and looked at it closely. " Someone has written a note in the margin of this page," he said, holding it up to the light. " It's written in pencil, very faintly. I can hardly make it out."

The children did make it out at last. " For more information, see page 87 of *Days of Smugglers*," the note said. The children looked at one another.

" That would be a book," said Alec, moving to the shelves. " Let's see who can find it first."

Hilary found it. She was always the sharpest of the three. It was a small book, bound in black, and the print was rather faded. She turned to page eighty-seven. The book was all about the district they were staying in, and on page eighty-seven was a description of the old caves. And then came something that excited the children very much. "Read it out, Ben, read it out!" cried Alec. "It's important."

So Ben read it out. "From a well-hidden opening between two old smuggler's caves is a curious passage, partly natural, partly man-made, probably by the smugglers themselves. This runs steadily upwards through the cliffs, and eventually stops not far from a little stream. A well-hidden hole leads upwards on to the moor. This was probably the way the smugglers used when they took their goods from the caves, over the country."

The children stared at one another, trembling with excitement. "So that's where the passage goes to!" said Alec. "My word—if only we could find the other end! Ben, have you any idea at all where it ends?"

"None at all," said Ben. "But it wouldn't be very difficult to find out! We know whereabouts the beginnings of the passage are—and if we follow a more or less straight line inland till we come to a stream on the moors, we might be able to spot the hole!"

"I say! Let's go now, at once, this very minute!" cried Hilary, shouting in her excitement.

"Shut up, silly," said Alec. "Do you want to tell everyone our secrets? It's almost dinner-time. We can't go now. But I vote we go immediatly afterwards!"

"Professor Rondel must have known all about those caves," said Ben thoughtfully. "I suppose he couldn't have anything to do with the queer people we overheard last night? No—that's too far-fetched. But the whole thing is very strange. I do hope we shall be able to find the entrance to the other end of that secret passage."

Mother called the children at that moment. " Dinner! " she cried. " Come along, bookworms, and have a little something to eat."

They were all hungry. They went to wash and make themselves tidy, and then sat down and ate a most enormous meal. Ben liked the children's mother very much. She talked and laughed, and he didn't feel a bit shy of her.

" You know, Alec and the girls really thought you were going after them with that knife of yours," she said.

Ben went red. " I did feel rather fierce that day," he said. " But it's awful when people come and spoil your secret places, isn't it? Now I'm glad they came, because they're the first friends I've ever had. We're having a fine time."

Mother looked out of the window as the children finished up the last of the jam tarts.

" It's clearing up," she said. " I think you all ought to go out. It will be very wet underfoot but you can put on your wellingtons. Why don't you go out on the moors for a change? "

" Oh *yes*, we will! " cried all four children at once. Mother was rather astonished.

" Well, you don't usually welcome any suggestion of walking in the wet," she said. " I believe you've got some sort of secret plan! "

But nobody told her what it was!

CHAPTER 7

GOOD HUNTING

AFTER DINNER the children put on their boots and
macs. They pulled on their sou'westers, and said
good-bye to their mother, and set off.

"Now for a good old hunt," said Ben. "First
let's go to the cliff that juts over my little cove.
Then we'll try to make out where the passage
begins underground and set off from that spot."

It wasn't long before they were over the cove.
The wind whipped their faces, and overhead the
clouds scudded by. Ben went to about the middle
of the cliff over the cove and stood there.

"I should say that the blocked-up passage runs
roughly under here," he said. "Now let's think.

Does it run quite straight from where it begins?
It curves a bit, doesn't it? "

" Yes, but it soon curved back again to the
blocked-up part," said Alec eagerly. " So you
can count it about straight to there. Let's walk in
a straight line from here till we think we've come
over the blocked-up bit."

They walked over the cliff inland, foot-deep in
purple heather. Then Ben stopped. " I reckon we
must just about be over the blocked-up bit," he
said. " Now listen—we've got to look for a stream.
There are four of us. We'll all part company and
go off in different directions to look for the stream.
Give a yell if you find one."

Soon Alec gave a yell. " There's a kind of
stream here! It runs along for a little way and
then disappears into a sort of little gully. I expect
it makes its way down through the cliff somewhere
and springs out into the sea. Would this be the
stream, do you think? "

Everyone ran to where Alec stood. Ben looked
down at the little brown rivulet. It was certainly
very small.

" It's been bigger once upon a time," he said,
pointing to where the bed was dry and wide.
" Maybe this is the one. There doesn't seem to be
another, anyway."

" We'll hunt about around here for an opening
of some sort," said Alec, his face red with excitement.

They all hunted about, and it was Hilary who
found it—quite by accident!

She was walking over the heather, her eyes
glancing round for any hole, when her foot went
right through into space! She had trodden on
what she thought was good solid ground, over
which heather grew—but almost at once she sank on
one knee as her foot went through some sort of hole!

" I say! My foot's gone through a hole here,"
she yelled. " Is it the one? It went right through
it. I nearly sprained my ankle."

The others came up. Ben pulled Hilary up and
then parted the heather to see. Certainly a big
hole was there—and certainly it seemed to go down
a good way.

The children tugged away at armfuls of heather
and soon got the tough roots out. The sides of the
hole fell away as they took out the heather. Ben
switched his torch on when it was fairly large.
There seemed to be quite a big drop down.

" We'd better slide down a rope," he said.

" We haven't got one," said Alec.

" I've got one round my waist," said Ben, and
undid a piece of strong rope from under his red
belt. A stout gorse bush stood not far off, and Ben
wound it round the strong stem at the bottom,
pricking himself badly but not seeming to feel it
at all.

" I'll go down," he said. He took hold of the
rope and lay down on the heather. Then he put
his legs into the hole and let himself go, holding
tightly to the rope. He slid into the hole, and went
a good way down.

" See anything? " yelled Alec.

"Yes. There *is* an underground channel here of some sort!" came Ben's voice, rather muffled. "I believe we're on to the right one. Wait a minute. I'm going to kick away a bit with my feet, and get some of the loose soil away."

After a bit Ben's voice came again, full of excitement.

"Come on down! There's a kind of underground channel, worn away by water. I reckon a stream must have run here at some time."

One by one the excited children slipped down the rope. They found what Ben had said—a kind of underground channel or tunnel plainly made by water of some kind in far-off days. Ben had his torch and the others had theirs. They switched them on.

Ben led the way. It was a curious path to take. Sometimes the roof was so low that the children had to crouch down, and once they had to go on hands and knees. Ben showed them the marks of tools in places where rocks jutted into the channel.

"Those marks were made by the smugglers, I reckon," he said. "They found this way and made it into a usable passage. They must have found it difficult getting some of their goods along here."

"I expect they unpacked those boxes we saw and carried the goods on their backs in bags or sacks," said Frances, seeing the picture clearly in her mind. "Ooooh—isn't it queer to think that heaps of smugglers have gone up this dark passage carrying smuggled goods years and years ago!"

They went on for a good way and then suddenly

"*Yes, there is an underground channel here of some sort!*"

came to an impassable bit where the roof had fallen in. They stopped.

" Well, here we are," said Ben, " we've come to the blocked-up part once more. Now the thing is—how far along is it blocked up—just a few yards, easy to clear—or a quarter of a mile? "

" I don't see how we can tell," said Alec. The four children stood and looked at the fallen stones and soil. It was most annoying to think they could get no farther.

" I know! " said Hilary suddenly. " I know! One of us could go in at the other end of the passage and yell. Then, if we can hear anything, we shall know the blockage isn't stretching very far! "

" Good idea, Hilary," said Ben, pleased. " Yes, that really *is* a good idea. I'd better be the one to go because I can go quickly. It'll take me a little time, so you must be patient. I shall yell loudly when I get up to the blocked bit, and then I shall knock on some stones with my spade. We did leave the spades there, didn't we? "

" We did," said Alec. " I say—this is getting awfully exciting, isn't it? "

Ben squeezed past the others and made his way up the channel. He climbed up the rope and sped off over the heather to the cliff-side. Down the narrow path he went, and jumped down into the cove.

Meanwhile, the others had sat down in the tunnel, to wait patiently for any noise they might hear.

" It will be terribly disappointing if we don't

hear anything," said Frances. They waited and waited. It seemed ages to them.

And then suddenly they heard something! It was Ben's voice, rather muffled and faint, but still quite unmistakable: "Hallooooooooo! Halloooooooo!"

Then came the sharp noise of a spade on rock: Crack! Crack! Crack!

"Hallooooooooo!" yelled back all three children, wildly excited. "Halloooooooo!"

"COME — AND — JOIN — ME!" yelled Ben's voice. "COME — AND — JOIN — ME!"

"COMING, COMING, COMING!" shouted Alec, Hilary and Frances, and all three scrambled back up to the entrance of the hole, swarming up the rope like monkeys.

They tore over the heather back to the cliff-side and almost fell down the steep path. Down into the cove on the sand—in the big cave—up on to the ledge—up the nail-studded hole—out on the ledge in the enormous cave—down to the rocky floor—over to the passage between the two caves —up the wall—and into the blocked-up passage where Ben was impatiently waiting for them.

"You *have* been quick," he cried. "I say—I could hear your voices quite well. The blocked piece can't stretch very far. Isn't that good? Do you feel able to tackle it hard now? If so, I believe we might clear it."

"I could tackle anything!" said Alec, taking off his mac. "I could tackle the cliff itself!"

Everyone laughed. They were all pleased and

excited, and felt able to do anything, no matter how hard it was.

" What's the time? " suddenly said Alec, when they had worked hard for a time, loosening the soil and filling the sacks. " Mother's expecting us in to tea, you know."

" It's a quarter-past four already," said Hilary, in dismay. " We must stop. But we'll come back after tea."

They sped off to their tea, and Mother had to cut another big plateful of bread and butter because they finished up every bit. Then off they went again, back to their exciting task.

" I say, I say, I say! " suddenly cried Alec, making everyone jump. " I've just thought of something marvellous."

" What? " asked everyone curiously.

" Well—if we can get this passage clear, we can come down it on Thursday night, from outside," said Alec. " We don't need to bother about the tides or anything. We can slip out at half-past eleven, go to the entrance on the moor and come down here and see what's happening! "

" Golly! I never thought of that! " cried Hilary.

Ben grinned. " That's fine," he said. " Yes— you can easily do that. You needn't disturb your mother at all. I think I'd better be here earlier, though, in case those people change their plans and come before they say. Though I don't think they will, because if they come in by motor boat, they'll need high tide to get their boat into the long cave."

The children went on working at the passage. Suddenly Ben gave a shout of joy.

" We're through! My spade went right through into nothing just then! Where's my torch? "

He shone it in front of him, and the children saw that he had spoken the truth. The light of the torch shone beyond into the other side of the passage! There was only a small heap of fallen earth to manage now.

" I think we'll finish this," said Alec, though he knew the girls were tired out. " I can't leave that little bit till to-morrow! You girls can sit down and have a rest. Ben and I can tackle this last bit. It will be easy."

It was. Before another half-hour had gone by, the passage was quite clear, and the children were able to walk up and down it from end to end. They felt pleased with themselves.

" Now we'll have to wait till Thursday," sighed Alec. " Gosh, what a long time it is—a whole day and a night and then another whole day. I simply can't wait! "

But they had to. They met Ben the next day and planned everything. They could hardly go to sleep on Wednesday night, and when Thursday dawned they were all awake as early as the sun.

CHAPTER 8

THURSDAY EVENING

THE DAY seemed very long indeed to the children
—but they had a lovely surprise in the afternoon.
Their father arrived, and with him he brought
their Uncle Ned. Mother rushed to the gate to meet
them as soon as she saw them, and the children
shouted for joy.

Uncle Ned said he could stay a day or two, and
Daddy said he would stay for a whole week.

" Where's Uncle Ned going to sleep? " asked
Alec. " In my room? "

In the ordinary way the boy would have been
very pleased at the idea of his uncle sleeping in the

same room with him—but to-night a grown-up might perhaps spoil things.

" Ned will have to sleep on the sofa in the sitting-room," said Mother. " I don't expect he will mind. He's had worse places to sleep in this war! "

Both Daddy and Uncle Ned were in the Army. It was lucky they had leave just when the children were on holiday. They could share a bit of it, too! All the children were delighted.

" I say—how are we going to slip out at half-past eleven to-night if Uncle Ned is sleeping in the sitting-room? " said Hilary, when they were alone. " We shall have to be jolly careful not to wake him! "

" Well, there's nothing for it but to creep through to the door," said Alec. " And if he does wake, we'll have to beg him not to tell tales of us."

The night came at last. The children went to bed as usual, but not one of them could go to sleep. They lay waiting for the time to pass—and it passed so slowly that once or twice Hilary thought her watch must have stopped. But it hadn't.

At last half-past eleven came—the time when they had arranged to leave, to go to meet Ben in the passage above the caves. Very quietly the children dressed. They all wore shorts, jerseys, their smugglers' hats, sashes and rubber boots. They stole down the stairs very softly. Not a stair creaked, not a child coughed.

The door of the sitting-room was a little open. Alec pushed it a little farther and put his head in. The room was dark. On the sofa Uncle Ned was lying, his regular breathing telling the children that he was asleep.

" He's asleep," whispered Alec, in a low voice. " I'll go across first and open the door. Then you two step across quietly to me. I'll shut the door after us."

The boy went across the room to the door. He opened it softly. He had already oiled it that day, by Ben's orders, and it made no sound. A streak of moonlight came in.

Silently the three children passed out and Alec shut the door. Just as they were going through the door, their uncle woke. He opened his eyes—and to his very great amazement saw the figures of the three children going quietly out of the open door. Then it shut.

Uncle Ned sat up with a jerk. Could he be dreaming? He opened the door and looked out. No—he wasn't dreaming. There were the three figures hurrying along to the moor in the moonlight. Uncle Ned was more astonished than he had ever been in his life before.

" Now what in the world do these kids think they are doing? " he wondered. " Little monkeys slipping out like this just before midnight. What are they up to? I'll go after them and see. Maybe they'll let me join in their prank, whatever it is. Anyway, Alec oughtn't to take his two sisters out at this time of night! "

Uncle Ned pulled on a mackintosh over his pyjamas and set out down the lane after the children. They had no idea he was some way behind them. They were thrilled because they thought they had got out so easily without being heard!

They got to the hole in the heather and by the light of their torch slid down the rope. Uncle Ned was more and more amazed as he saw one child after another slide down and disappear completely. He didn't know any hole was there, of course. He found it after a time and decided to go down it himself.

Meanwhile, the children were half-way down the passage. There they met Ben, and whispered in excitement to him. " We got out without being seen—though our uncle was sleeping on the sofa near the door! Ben, have you seen or heard anything yet? "

" Not a thing," said Ben. " But they should be here soon, because it's almost midnight and the tide is full."

They all went down to the end of the passage, and jumped down to stand at the end of the long, narrow cave. This was now full of water, and the waves rushed up it continually.

" Easy enough to float any motor boat right in," said Ben. " I wonder what they're bringing."

" Listen! " said Hilary suddenly. " I'm sure I can hear something."

" It's the chug-chug-chug of that motor boat again," whispered Alec, a shiver going down his back. He wasn't frightened, but it was all so exciting he couldn't help trembling. The girls were the same. Their knees shook a little. Only Ben was quite still and fearless.

"Now don't switch your torches on by mistake, for goodness' sake," whispered Ben, as the chugging noise came nearer. "We'll stay here till we see the boat coming into the long channel of this cave then we'll hop up into the passage and listen hard."

The motor boat came nearer and nearer. Then as it nosed gently into the long cave with its deep inlet of water, the engine was shut off.

"Now we must go," said Ben, and the four children turned. They climbed up into the passage above the caves and stood there, listening.

People got out of the motor boat, which was apparently tied up to some rock. Torches were switched on. Ben, who was leaning over the hole from the passage, counted three people going into the big cave—two men and a woman. One of the men seemed somehow familiar to him, but he was gone too quickly for Ben to take a second look.

"Well, here we are," said a voice from the enormous cave below. "I will leave you food and drink, and you will wait here till it is safe to go inland. You have maps to show you how to go. You know what to do. Do it well. Come back here and the motor boat will fetch you a week from now."

The children listening above could not make out at all what was happening. Who were the people? And what were the two of them to do? Alec pressed hard by Ben to listen better. His foot touched a pebble and set it rolling down into the space between the caves. Before he could stop himself he gave a low cry of annoyance.

There was instant silence in the cave. Then the first voice spoke again very sharply: " What was that? Did you hear anything? "

A wave roared up the narrow cave nearby and made a great noise. Whilst the splashing was going on Ben whispered to Alec: " Move back up the passage, quick! You idiot, they heard you! They'll be looking for us in a minute! "

The children hurried back along the passage as quietly as they could, their hearts beating painfully. And half-way along it they bumped into somebody!

Hilary screamed. Frances almost fainted with fright. Then the Somebody took their arms and said:

" Now what in the world are you kids doing here at this time of night? "

" Uncle Ned, oh, Uncle Ned! " said Hilary, in a faint voice. " Oh, it's marvellous to have a grown-up just at this very minute to help us! Uncle Ned, something very queer is going on. Tell him, Alec."

Alec told his astonished uncle very quickly all that had happened. He listened without a word, and then spoke in a sharp, stern voice that the children had never heard before.

" They're spies! They've come over from the coast of Ireland. It's just opposite here, you know. Goodness knows what they're going to do—some dirty work, I expect. We've got to stop them. Now let me think. How can we get them? Can they get away from the caves except by motor boat? "

" Only up this passage, until the tide goes down," said Ben. " Sir—listen to me. I could slip down

the hole and cast off the motor boat by myself. I
know how to start it up. I believe I could do it.
Then you could hold this passage, couldn't you,
and send Alec and the girls back to get their father.
You'd have to get somebody to keep guard outside
the cave as soon as the tide goes down, in case they
try to escape round the cliffs."

"Leave that to me," said Uncle Ned grimly.
"Can you really get away in that motor boat? If
you can, you'll take their only means of escape.
Well, go and try. Good luck to you. You're a
brave lad!"

Ben winked at the others, who were staring at
him open-mouthed. Then he slipped along down
the passage again until he came to the opening.
He stood there listening before he let himself down
into the space between the caves. It was plain that
the people there had come to the conclusion that
the noise they had heard was nothing to worry
about, for they were talking together. There was
the clink of glasses as the boy dropped down quietly
to the floor below the passage.

"They're wishing each other good luck!" said
the boy to himself, with a grin. He went to the
motor boat, which was gently bobbing up and down
as waves ran under it up the inlet of water in the
cave. He climbed quietly in. He felt about for the
rope that was tied round a rock, and slipped it
loose. The next wave took the boat down with it,
and as soon as he dared, Ben started up the engine
to take her out of the deep channel in the cave.

He was lucky in getting the boat out fairly

quickly. As soon as the engine started up, there came a shout from the cave, and Ben knew that the two men there had run to see what was happening. He ducked in case there was any shooting. He guessed that the men would be desperate when they saw their boat going.

He got the boat clear, and swung her out on the water that filled the cove. The boy knew the coast almost blindfold, and soon the little motor boat was chug-chug-chugging across the open sea towards the beach where a little jetty ran out, and where Ben could tie her up. He was filled with glee. It was marvellous to think he had beaten those men—and that woman, too, whoever she was. Spies! Well—now they knew what British boys and girls could do!

He wondered what the others were doing. He felt certain that Alec and the girls were even now speeding up the passage, climbing out through the heather and racing back home to waken their father.

And that is exactly what they *were* doing! They had left their uncle in the passage—and in his hand was his loaded revolver. No one could escape by that passage, even if they knew of it.

"Tell your father what you have told me, and tell him Ben has taken the boat away," he said. "I want men to guard the outer entrance of the caves as soon as the tide goes down. I'll remain here to guard this way of escape. Go quickly!"

CHAPTER 9

THINGS MOVE QUICKLY

ALEC AND the two girls left their uncle and stumbled up the dark passage, lighting their way by their small torches. All three were trembling with excitement. It seemed suddenly a very serious thing that was happening. Spies! Who would have thought of that?

They went on up the passage. Soon they came to the place where the roof fell very low indeed, and down they went on their hands and knees to crawl through the low tunnel.

"I don't like that bit much," said Frances, when they were through it. "I shall dream about that! Come on—we can stand upright again now. Whatever do you suppose Daddy and Mother will say?"

"I can't imagine," said Alec. "All I know is that it's a very lucky thing for us that Daddy and Uncle happened to be here now. Golly—didn't I jump when we bumped into Uncle Ned in this passage!"

"I screamed," said Hilary, rather ashamed of herself. "But honestly I simply couldn't help it. It was awful to bump into sombebody strange like that in the darkness. But wasn't I glad when I heard Uncle Ned's voice!"

"Here we are at last," said Alec, as they came to where the rope hung down the hole. "I'll go up first and then give you two girls a hand. Give me a heave, Hilary."

Hilary heaved him up and he climbed the rope quickly, hand over hand, glad that he had been so good at gym at school. You never knew when things would come in useful!

He lay down on the heather and helped the girls up. They stood out on the moor in the moonlight, getting back their breath, for it wasn't easy to haul themselves up the rope.

"Now come on," said Hilary. "We haven't any time to lose. I shouldn't be surprised if those spies know about the passage and make up their minds to try it. We don't want to leave Uncle Ned too long. After all, it's three against one."

They tore over the heather, and came to the

sandy lane where Sea Cottage shone in the moonlight. They went in at the open door and made their way to their parents' bedroom. Alec hammered on the door, and then went in.

His father and mother were sitting up in astonishment. They switched on the light and stared at the three children, all fully dressed as they were.

"What's the meaning of this?" asked their father. But before he could say a word more the three children began to pour out their story. At first their parents could not make out what they were talking about, and their mother made the girls stop talking so that Alec could tell the tale.

"But this is unbelievable!" said their father, dressing as quickly as possible. "Simply unbelievable! Is Ned really down a secret passage, holding three spies at bay? And Ben has gone off with their motor boat? Am I dreaming?"

"No, Daddy, you're not," said Alec. "It's all quite true. We kept everything a secret till to-night, because secrets are such fun. We didn't know that anything serious was up till to-night, really. Are you going to get help?"

"I certainly am," said Daddy. He went to the telephone downstairs and was soon on to the nearest military camp. He spoke to a most surprised commanding officer, who listened in growing amazement.

"So you must send a few men over as quickly as possible," said Daddy. "The children say there are three men in the caves—or rather, two men and one woman—but there may be more, of course—

and more may arrive. We can't tell. Hurry, won't you?"

He put down the receiver of the telephone and turned to look at the waiting children. "Now let me see," he said thoughtfully. "I shall want one of you to take me to where Ned is—and I must leave someone behind to guide the soldiers down to the cove. They must be there to guard the entrance to the caves, so that if the spies try to escape by the beach, they will find they can't. Alec, you had better come with me. Frances and Hilary, you can go with Mother and the soldiers, when they come, and show them the way down the cliff and the entrance to the caves. Come along, Alec."

The two set off. Alec talked hard all the way, for there was a great deal to tell. His father listened in growing astonishment. Really, you never knew what children were doing half the time!

"I suppose your mother thought you were playing harmless games of smugglers," he said, "and all the time you were on the track of dangerous spies! Well, well, well!"

"We didn't really know they were spies till to-night," said Alec honestly. "It was all a game at first. Look, Daddy—here's the hole. We have to slide down this rope."

"This really is a weird adventure," said his father, and down the rope he went. Alec followed him. Soon they were standing beside Uncle Ned, who was still in the passage, his revolver in his hand.

"There's been a lot of excited talking," he said

in a low voice to his brother, " and I think they've been trying to find a way out. But the tide is still very high, and they daren't walk out on the sand yet. If they don't know of this passage, they won't try it, of course—but we'd better stay here in case they do. When are the soldiers coming? "

" At once," said Daddy. " I've left the two girls behind to guide them down to the cove. Then they will hide, and guard the entrance to the caves, that is as soon as the tide goes down enough."

" Do the spies know you're here, Uncle Ned? " asked Alec, in a low voice.

" No," said his uncle. " They know someone has gone off with their motor boat, but that's all they know. What about creeping down to the end of the passage to see if we can overhear anything? They might drop a few secrets! "

The three of them crept down to the end of the passage, and leaned out over the hole that led down to the space between the two caves. They could hear the waves still washing up the narrow channel in the long cave.

The two men and the woman were talking angrily. " Who could have known we were here? Someone has given the game away! No one but ourselves and the other three knew what we were planning to do."

" Is there no other way out? " said a man's impatient voice, very deep and foreign. " Rondel, you know all these caves and passages—or so you said. How did the old smugglers get their goods away? There must have been a land path they used."

"There was," said the other man. "There is a passage above this cave that leads on to the moors. But as far as I know it is completely blocked up."

"As far as you know!" said the other man, in a scornful voice. "Haven't you found out? What do you suppose you are paid for, Rondel? Aren't you paid for letting us know any well-hidden caves on this coast? Where is this passage? Do you know?"

"Yes, I know," said Rondel. "It's above this one, and the entrance to it is just between this cave and the one we used for the motor boat. We have to climb up a little way. I've never been up it myself, because I heard it was blocked up by a roof-fall years ago. But we can try it and see."

"We'd better get back up the passage a bit," whispered Alec's father. "If they come up here, we may have trouble. Get up to that bit where the big rock juts out and the passage goes round it. We can get behind that and give them a scare. They'll shoot if they see us. I don't want to shoot them if I can help it, for I've a feeling they will be more useful alive than dead!"

Very silently the three went back up the passage to where a rock jutted out and the way went round it. They crouched down behind the rock and waited, their torches switched off. Alec heard their breathing and it sounded very loud. But they had to breathe! He wondered if Daddy and Uncle could hear his heart beating, because it seemed to make a very loud thump just then!

Meanwhile, the three spies were trying to find the entrance to the passage. Rondel had a powerful torch, and he soon found the hole that led to the ledge where the secret passage began.

"Here it is!" he said. "Look—we can easily get up there. I'll go first."

Alec heard a scrambling noise as the man climbed up. Then he pulled up the other two. They all switched on their torches and the dark passage was lighted up brightly.

"It seems quite clear," said the other man. "I should think we could escape this way. You go ahead, Rondel. We'll follow. I can't see any sign of it being blocked up, I must say! This is a bit of luck."

They went on up the passage talking. They went slowly, and Alec and the others could hear their footsteps and voices coming gradually nearer. Alec's heart beat painfully and he kept swallowing something in his throat. The excitement was almost too much for him to bear.

The three spies came almost up to the jutting-out rock. And then they got the shock of their lives! Alec's father spoke in a loud, stern voice that made Alec jump.

"Halt! Come another step, and we'll shoot!"

The spies halted at once in a panic. They switched off their torches.

"Who's there?" came Rondel's voice.

Nobody answered. The spies talked together in low voices and decided to go back the way they had come. They were not risking going round that rock! They didn't know how many people were there. It was plain that somebody knew of their plans and meant to capture them.

Alec heard the three making their way quietly back down the passage.

"Daddy! I expect they think the tide will soon be going down and they hope to make their escape by way of the beach," whispered Alec. "I hope the soldiers will be there in time."

"Don't you worry about that!" said his father. "As soon as the tide washes off the beach, it will be full of soldiers."

"I wish I could be there," said Alec longingly. "I don't expect the spies will come up here again."

"Well, you can go and see what's happening if you like," said Daddy. "Your uncle and I will stay here—but you can see if the soldiers have arrived and if the girls are taking them down to the cove."

Alec was delighted. More excitement for him, after all! He went up the passage and swarmed up the rope out of the entrance-hole. He sped over the moor to the cottage.

But no one was there. It was quite empty. "I suppose the soldiers have arrived and Mother and the girls have taken them to the cove," thought Alec. "Yes—there are big wheel-marks in the road—a lorry has been here. Oh—there it is, in the shade of those trees over there. I'd better hurry or I'll miss the fun!"

Off he dashed to the cliff-edge, and down the narrow, steep path. Where were the others? Waiting in silence down on the beach? Alec nearly fell down the steep path trying to hurry! What an exciting night!

CHAPTER 10

THE END OF IT ALL

JUST AS Alec was scrambling down the steep cliff, he heard the sound of a low voice from the top. "Is that you, Alec?"

Alec stopped. It was Ben's voice. "Ben!" he whispered in excitement. "Come on down. You're just in time. How did you get here?"

Ben scrambled down beside him. "I thought it was you," he said. "I saw you going over the edge of the cliff as I came up the lane. What's happened?"

Alec told him. Ben listened in excitement.

"So they know there's someone in the secret passage," he said. "They'll just have to try to escape by the beach then! Well, they'll be over-powered there, no doubt about that. I tied up the motor boat by the jetty, Alec. It's a real beauty—small but very powerful. It's got a lovely engine. Then I raced back to see if I could be in at the end."

"Well, you're just in time," said Alec. "I'm going to hop down on to the beach now and see where the others are."

"Be careful," Ben warned him. "The soldiers won't know it's you, and may take a pot-shot at you."

That scared Alec. He stopped before he jumped down on to the sand.

"Well, I think maybe we'd better stay here then," he said. "We can see anything that happens from here, can't we? Look, the tide is going down nicely now. Where do you suppose the others are, Ben?"

"I should think they are somewhere on the rocks that run round the cove," said Ben, looking carefully round. "Look, Alec—there's something shining just over there—see? I guess that's a gun. We can't see the man holding it—but the moon-light just picks out a shiny bit of his gun."

"I hope the girls and Mother are safe," said Alec.

"You may be sure they are," said Ben. "I wonder what the three spies are doing now. I guess they are waiting till the tide is low enough for them to come out."

At that very moment Rondel was looking out of the big cave to see if it was safe to try and escape over the beach. He was not going to try to go up the cliff-path, for he felt sure there would be someone at the top. Their only hope lay in slipping round the corner of the cove and making their way up the cliff some way off. Rondel knew the coast by heart, and if he only had the chance he felt certain he could take the others to safety.

The tide was going down rapidly. The sand was very wet and shone in the moonlight. Now and again a big wave swept up the beach, but the power behind it was gone. It could not dash anyone against the rocks now. Rondel turned to his two companions and spoke to them in a low voice.

"Now's our chance. We shall have to try the beach whilst our enemies think the tide is still high. Take hold of Gretel's hand, Otto, in case a wave comes. Follow me. Keep as close to the cliff as possible in case there is a watcher above."

The three of them came silently out of the big cave. Its entrance lay in darkness and they looked like deep black shadows as they moved quietly to the left of the cave. They made their way round the rocks, stopping as a big wave came splashing up the smooth sand. It swept round their feet, but no higher. Then it ran back down the sand again to the sea, and the three moved on once more.

Then a voice rang out in the moonlight: "We have you covered! There is no escape this way! Hands up!"

Rondel had his revolver in his hand in a moment and guns glinted in the hands of the others, too. But they did not know where their enemies were.

The rocks lay in black shadows, and no one could be seen.

"There are men all round this cove," said the voice. "You cannot escape. Put your hands up and surrender. Throw your revolvers down, please."

Rondel spoke to the others in a savage voice. He was in a fierce rage, for all his plans were ruined. It seemed as if he were urging the others to fight. But they were wiser than Rondel. The other man threw his revolver down on the sand and put his hands above his head. The woman did the same. They glinted there like large silver shells.

"Hands up, you!" commanded a voice. Rondel shouted something angry in a foreign language and then threw his gun savagely at the nearest rocks. It hit them and the trigger was struck. The revolver went off with a loud explosion that echoed round and round the little cove and made everyone, Rondel as well, jump violently.

"Stand where you are," said a voice. And out from the shadow of the rocks came a soldier in the uniform of an officer. He walked up to the three spies and had a look at them. He felt them all over to see if there were any more weapons hidden about them. There were none.

He called to his men. "Come and take them."

Four men stepped out from the rocks around the cove. Alec and Ben leapt down on to the sand. Mother and the two girls came out from their hiding-place in a small cave. Ben ran up to the spies. He peered into the face of one of the men.

" I know who this is! " he cried. " It's Professor Rondel, who lived in Sea Cottage. I've seen him hundreds of times! He didn't have many friends— only two or three men who came to see him sometimes."

" Oh," said the officer, staring with interest at Ben. " Well, we'll be very pleased to know who the two or three men were. You'll be very useful to us, my boy. Now then—quick march! Up the cliff we go and into the lorry! The sooner we get these three into a safe place the better."

Alec's father and uncle appeared at that moment. They had heard the sound of the shot when Rondel's revolver struck the rock and went off, and they had come to see what was happening. Alec ran to them and told them.

" Good work! " said Daddy. " Three spies caught—and maybe the others they work with, too, if Ben can point them out. Good old Smuggler Ben! "

The three spies were put into the lorry and the driver climbed up behind the wheel. The officer saluted and took his place. Then the lorry rumbled off into the moonlit night. The four children watched it go, their eyes shining.

" This is the most thrilling night I've ever had in my life," said Alec, with a sigh. " I don't suppose I'll ever have a more exciting one, however long I live. Golly, my heart did beat fast when we were hiding in the cave. It hurt me."

" Same here," said Hilary. " Oh, Daddy—you didn't guess what you were in for, did you, when you came home yesterday? "

" I certainly didn't," said Daddy, putting his arm round the two girls and pushing them towards the house. " Come along—you'll all be tired out. It must be nearly dawn! "

" Back to Professor Rondel's own house! " said Alec. " Isn't it funny! He got all his information from his books—and we found some of it there, too. We'll show you if you like, Daddy."

" Not to-night," said Daddy firmly. " To-night —or rather this morning, for it's morning now— you are going to bed, and to sleep. No more excitement, please! You will have plenty again to-morrow, for you'll have to go over to the police and to the military camp to tell all you know."

Well, that was an exciting piece of news, too. The children went indoors, Ben with them, for Mother said he had better sleep with Alec for the rest of the night.

Soon all four children were in their beds, feeling certain that they would never, never be able to go to sleep for one moment.

But it wasn't more than two minutes before they were all sound asleep, as Mother saw when she peeped into the two bedrooms. She went to join Daddy and Uncle Ned.

" Well, I'd simply no idea what the children were doing," she told them. " I was very angry with them one night when they came home late because they were caught by the tide when they were exploring those caves. They kept their secret well."

"They're good kids," said Daddy, with a yawn. "Well, let's go to sleep, too. Ned, I hope you'll be able to drop off on the sofa again."

"I could drop off on the kitchen stove, I'm so tired!" said Ned.

Soon the whole household slept soundly, and did not wake even when the sun came slanting in at the windows. They were all tired out.

They had a late breakfast, and the children chattered nineteen to the dozen as they ate porridge and bacon and eggs. It all seemed amazingly wonderful to them now that it was over. They couldn't help feeling rather proud of themselves.

"I must go," said Ben, when he had finished an enormous breakfast. "My uncle is expecting me to go out fishing with him this morning. He'll be angry because I'm late."

But before Ben could go, a messenger on a motor bike arrived, asking for the four children to go over to the police station at once. The police wanted to know the names of the men with whom Professor Rondel had made friends. This was very important, because unless they knew the names at once, the men might hear of Rondel's capture and fly out of the country.

So off went the four children, and spent a most exciting time telling and retelling their story from the very beginning. The inspector of the police listened carefully, and when everything had been told, and notes taken, he leaned back and looked at the children, his eyes twinkling.

"Well, we have reason to be very grateful to you four smugglers," he said. "We shall probably catch the whole nest of spies operating in this part of the country. We suspected it—but we had no idea who the ringleader was. It was Rondel, of course. He was bringing men and women across from Ireland—spies, of course—and taking them about the country either to get information useful to the enemy, or to wreck valuable buildings. He was using the old smugglers' caves to hide his friends in. We shall comb the whole coast now."

"Can we help you?" asked Ben eagerly. "I know most of the caves, sir. And we can show you Rondel's books, where all the old caves are described. He's got dozens of them."

"Good!" said the inspector. "Well, that's all for to-day. You will hear from us later. There will be a little reward given to you for services to your country!"

The children filed out, talking excitedly. A little reward! What could it be?

"Sometimes children are given watches as a reward," said Alec, thinking of a newspaper report he had read. "We might get a watch each."

"I hope we don't," said Hilary, "because I've already got one—though it doesn't keep very good time."

But the reward wasn't watches. It was something much bigger than that. Can you possibly guess what it was?

It was the little motor boat belonging to the spies! When the children heard the news, they could hardly believe their ears. But it was quite true. There lay the little motor boat, tied up to the jetty, and on board was a police officer with instructions to hand it over to the four children.

"Oh—thank you!" said Alec, hardly able to speak. "Thank you very much. Oh, Ben—oh, Ben—isn't it marvellous!"

It *was* marvellous! It was a beautiful little boat with a magnificent engine. It was called *Otto*.

"That won't do," said Hilary, looking at the name. "We'll have that painted out at once. What shall we call our boat? It must be a very good name—something that will remind us of our adventure!"

"I know—I know!" yelled Alec. "We'll call it *Smuggler Ben*, of course—and good old Ben shall be the captain, and we'll be his crew."

So *Smuggler Ben* the boat was called, and everyone agreed that it was a really good name. The children have a wonderful time in it. You should see them chug-chug-chugging over the sea at top speed, the spray flying high in the air! Aren't they lucky!

THE END

Have you read all the adventures in the "Mystery" series
by Enid Blyton?

THE ROCKINGDOWN MYSTERY

Staying at Rockingdown Hall, Roger, Diana, Snubby and
Barney hear strange noises in the cellars. Barney goes to
investigate and makes a very startling discovery . . .

THE RILLOBY FAIR MYSTERY

Valuable papers have disappeared – the Green Hands Gang
has struck again! Which of Barney's workmates at the circus
is responsible? The four friends turn detectives – and have to
tackle a dangerous criminal.

THE RUBADUB MYSTERY

Who is the enemy agent at the top-secret submarine harbour?
Roger, Diana, Snubby and Barney are determined to find out –
and find themselves in a most exciting mystery.

THE RING O'BELLS MYSTERY

Eerie events have been happening at deserted Ring O'Bells
Hall – and they spark off another mystery for the four friends
to solve.

THE RAT-A-TAT MYSTERY

When the big knocker on the ancient door of Rat-a-tat House
bangs by itself in the middle of the night, it heralds a series
of very peculiar happenings – and another action-packed
adventure for Roger, Diana, Snubby and Barney.

THE RAGAMUFFIN MYSTERY

"This is going to be the most exciting holiday we've ever had,"
said Roger – and little does he know how true his words will
prove when he and his three friends go to Merlin's Cove and
discover the hideout of a gang of thieves.

Armada

The Hardy Boys Mystery Stories
by Franklin W. Dixon

Look out for these thrilling new mysteries which will be coming soon in Armada.

The Mummy Case (61)

The Hardys are en route for Egypt – as chaperones to a mummy! But some cut-throat thieves are out to seize the priceless relic. In a deadly war of nerves, the Hardy Boys fight their enemies under the burning desert sun.

The Mystery of Smugglers Cove (62)

When a valuable painting is stolen, the Hardy Boys are determined to catch the thieves. But the trail of clues soon leads them to the steamy swamps of Florida – and to a deadly encounter with some man-eating alligators!

The Stone Idol (63)

The strange disappearance of an ancient stone statue begins a hair-raising new adventure for the Hardys. But their investigations lead them into a sinister trap – in the freezing wilderness of the Antarctic.

Armada

The Nancy Drew Mystery Stories
by Carolyn Keene

Don't miss the latest exciting adventures in this action-packed series!

The Secret in the Old Lace (53)
A strange mystery from the past takes Nancy to Belgium in search of fabulous treasure. But a secret enemy lurks in the winding streets – an enemy who is determined to destroy her . . .

Coming soon

The Greek Symbol Mystery (54)
Nancy's life is in danger when she goes to Greece on the trail of a ruthless gang of art smugglers. Will she manage to outwit her enemies, or will the riddle of the ancient Byzantine mask remain unsolved forever . . . ?

Armada

LINDA CRAIG
MYSTERIES

by ANN SHELDON

Now there's a thrilling new mystery series in Armada.

Linda Craig loves horses – and adventure! Together, she and her beautiful palomino pony, Chica D'Oro, find themselves caught up in all kinds of dangerous escapades – chasing cut-throat horse thieves through underground caverns, roaring down mountain passes after death-dealing smugglers, treasure-hunting in the burning desert – and much more. Make sure you don't miss Linda's first two action-packed adventures.

1. **The Palomino Mystery**
2. **The Clue on the Desert Trail**

Coming soon
3. **The Secret of Rancho del Sol**
4. **The Mystery of Horseshoe Canyon**

If you like Nancy Drew, you'll love Linda Craig!

Armada

has a whole shipload
of exciting books for you

Armadas are chosen by children all over the world.
They're designed to fit your pocket, and your pocket
money too – and they make terrific presents for friends.
They're colourful, exciting, and there are hundreds of
titles to choose from – thrilling mysteries, spooky ghost
stories, hilarious joke books, brain-teasing quizzes and
puzzles, fascinating hobby books, stories about ponies and
schools – and many, many more. Armada has something
for everyone.

Book
Tokens

**Give them
the pleasure of choosing**

Book Tokens can be bought
and exchanged at most
bookshops.

Armada